Temp

Life in the Stagnant Lane

Scott Nagele

Because the difference between temporary and permanent is a simple matter of time.

October, 2011

Temp

Life in the Stagnant Lane

Acknowledgements

The author owes many thanks to Janet Harvey-Clark and Lawrence Andrews, two skilled readers who have made this book much better than it otherwise would have been. Thanks is also richly deserved by LaRay and Jacob, whose love and support is irreplaceable.

About the Author

Scott Nagele lives in Michigan with his wife, LaRay, and son, Jacob. Over the years, he has worked as a temp, as well as in retail management, and in the world of higher education. His short fiction has been published in literary reviews, including the Berkeley Fiction Review. His previous novel is Wasted Moons: Man vs. 1997. Scott Nagele can be reached at snblues@aol.com.

Cover design by The Nagele Group

This book is a work of fiction. The characters, places, and events depicted are imaginary.

Contents:

1.
A Senseless Crime

A lady stole my shopping cart in the grocery store. She's probably a very nice lady, most of the time, but that won't stop me from thinking of her as a thief.

I turned my back on the cart to take a look at some lettuce when I saw a flash of navy blue out of the corner of my eye. It passed right behind me, close enough to make me turn around. There it went—my cart, swiped by a middle-aged thief in business casual.

She turned her head from side to side, as if she were interested in the produce, pretending she didn't know anything about a crime having been committed. She didn't stop for any onions though. She just boogied right along until she could disappear down the canned goods aisle. I know what you're thinking: maybe she thought it was an abandoned cart. Well, you didn't see the way she wove through that produce section to get away. She probably had the escape route planned out in advance. She knew exactly what she was doing.

On top of that, all the heads of lettuce were disgusting.

Even so, I didn't press charges.

It's amazing how being violated makes you take stock of your life. I think I'm doing okay; then I become the victim of a senseless crime. The next thing I know, I'm in full self-analysis mode. My problem is that my whole philosophy of life is bi-polar. There's a part of me that wants to work hard and be ambitious—

leave my mark on the world—that sort of thing. I should try to be the best, or at least pretty good, at something.

I pass among successful people every day; I suspect some of them own cuff links. I listen to what these people say, and you know, I can't remember one time when I thought, "Wow, that guy's a genius!" So I figure I'm just as smart as any of these success stories. Why not get myself an advanced degree, get successful, and leave my mark on the world? A degree in what though? I still have no clue what I want to do with my life. I've never heard of a Ph.D. in Finding Your Way. If they offered that degree, I'd rush right out and get one. Meanwhile, am I supposed to go out and get a degree and work my butt off being successful in something I may not even like? I can just hear them now: "Did you get a load of that Gary Gray? He has the biggest, golden-est cuff links in the whole Mindlessly Shuffling Paperwork Department." Of course, before the doctorate, I'd have to earn a master's degree. I'm still looking for an institution that offers a graduate program in Knowing Your Ass from a Hole in the Ground.

That leads me to the other side of my bi-polar outlook: Why bother? Why not just enjoy life as it is? Sure, I'm not exactly living in luxury, but I'm not sleeping under an overpass either. Why should I kill myself trying to be a success at a career picked out of a hat? In a hundred years, I'll be dead, and all that struggle and pain, and whatever else it took to make it big, would have gotten me exactly as deep into the ground as everyone else my age. I say, hey, if something came easy to you, and you lucked into a good job doing it, and you were happy, great. But if you had to scratch and claw to make a living at it, and worked hard and sacrificed, well, where are you now? You're dead, that's where, just like the lucky bastard who had an easy time of it, only he enjoyed his life while you were busy dedicating yours. Yeah, everybody wants to prove that they have what it takes to make it big, but when I get my headline, I don't want it to say, "Local Boy Makes Good, Dies of Trying Soon After."

I have what's left of the wind taken out of my ambition whenever I take a walk through the library. Most of the books there never get touched. Somebody poured years into each book, agonizing over whether they should use a comma here, or hyphenate that word. These people gave themselves migraines, slaving over the damned things. Now they're dead, and their creations sit gathering dust. This was their great footprint. This makes them immortal. They might better have spent their time relaxing and enjoying themselves—drinking beer, having sex, making babies. At least one of their grandkids might rob a bank and keep the family name in the papers.

So that's the motivational problem I have. It doesn't explain why that lady stole my shopping cart.

I was really peeved when she swiped it. I wasn't thinking at all about how insignificant that cart would be in a hundred years. It was all about the here and now, and maybe the next half hour. Nothing makes you appreciate life like being the victim of a crime.

My girlfriend thinks I should go back to school and get an accounting degree. This is what she doesn't get: just because I can add and subtract numbers, and most times the sums come out right, doesn't mean I want to spend my life adding and subtracting. Isn't accounting just the process of taking a big number, smashing it up into a lot of smaller numbers, mixing those little numbers around, then pasting them all back to see if they can be pieced together into the big number again? Instead of doing all that work, hoping to end up just where they started, it seems like reasonable people would set the big number in a safe place and leave well enough alone.

If I had gotten my temp assignment at any other place besides the accounting department at Appalachian Downslope

College, Gwen never would have thought of me as a potential accountant. But I had to land there, where none of the permanent employees can make their sums come out right. Consequently, I look like an accounting genius when I'm really just a guy who's okay at arithmetic.

I don't even know how long I'll be able to keep this assignment. People around the college are starting to see who's making the math errors and who's not. The permanent employees don't like that. It's obvious that they would be more comfortable without me around. Then, people could go back to thinking that math only works out right 30 or 40 percent of the time, and everybody in the accounting department could relax again. Some of them have tried to discourage me by attempting to make me look stupid. They'll cite some big accounting rule that they've had in their back pocket for years, not knowing what to do with it. True, I don't know the official accounting rules, but then I'm not an accountant and I never claimed to be one. I'm just a temp with passable math skills. They expect me to get embarrassed when I don't know what they're talking about, but I shrug it off and say stuff like, "That sounds like a damned fine rule. The world would be a better place if we all could learn to live by it."

There's a lot of stress that comes with being a temp. You don't know how long you'll have a job. My situation is starting to worry the accounting manager. People are beginning to expect fewer errors in the output of his department. He can't let expectations get too high. Then, he'd have to hire me, or somebody else who can do reliable arithmetic, full time. To do that, he'd have to let go one of the permanent employees, but all of them know too much about him. Let's just say the man has certain appetites, some of which have led him into compromising positions. It could be really difficult for him to fire somebody who knows the slimy details of these instances, especially if they participated in some of them.

Even if I wanted to dig up the dirt on my boss that could save my job, no one in the department is going to share with me. They fear that I will begin to gain my own leverage. Then, nobody's safe, because when everybody has immunity, nobody is immune. They scurry around fact checking with each other while trying to keep the same nuggets of gossip from me. Sometimes I feel guilty for being the cause of such turmoil. There are even moments when I think I should start making subtraction errors, just to ease the tension. But I can't bring myself to do it. I've got my pride, such as it is.

Isn't it clever how I call it the stress of being a temp, when it's really the stress of going nowhere in life, and realizing it? If I could just get my act together and go get a master's in some crazy thing, everybody could take a deep breath. It's a curse to be a person who can do sums, but can't get your shit together, because then you're perfectly equipped to calculate just exactly how far behind you have let yourself fall.

Falling behind in the rat race is nothing to cry about though. There are worse things than a little financial struggle here and there. Look, I have a great girlfriend who can see through my surface lack of success to the hidden potential within. Actually, I have no idea what she sees in me, but she's cute, and we have a great sex life; and when you think of all the successful people who must have really miserable sex lives, well, there are worse things than falling a little behind.

Gwen splits her time between school and the book store. Between us, we manage to pay the rent on our little apartment and subscribe to basic cable. We agreed that neither of us will accept any financial support from our parents. I'm a self-made man and Gwen's a self-made woman, only she got self-made after she moved in with me and her parents cut her off. It worked right into our plan for self-sufficiency.

In two years Gwen will get her bachelor's. Then she'll be

5

on par with me and ready to zoom ahead. I guess that will give her some sort of perceived right to get on my case about getting a real job or more education. She could even throw me over altogether. I should probably marry her before then. Meanwhile, I'm monitoring the situation closely. There aren't many girls out there who can see through the outer veneer of failure quite so clearly as she does. Of those, I doubt many are as cute as she is. If there's one thing you have to give me credit for it's that I appreciate what I have, and I'm going to do whatever it takes to keep it, if a time comes when I have to do something special to keep it. Meantime, as I said, I'm watching things closely.

I'm not saying that Gwen is the type to push me into anything. But she'll want children some day, and those little rascals cost money. On the other hand, she's an English major, so I'm not sure how much traction she'd get pushing anybody anywhere. Don't get me wrong: she's incredibly smart. In fact, she's a genius. If you'd ever seen how quickly she can tear through one of those 200-year-old, 800-page novels, and still get the point of the thing, you'd know just what a genius she is. But she is an English major. So we'll see where that leads. I mean, she already works in a book store.

Then again, Gwen doesn't get shopping carts stolen from right under her nose. At least she claims she doesn't. When I told her about the incident, she made it into a big scandal, letting that thieving cart swiper off scot-free and making me out to be the culprit. She let out a shocked and disappointed gasp. "You turned your back on your cart? What if the baby had been in that cart?"

"I don't have a baby," I told her, but I had to think about it first to make sure. She has this way of making you accept the premise of her argument.

"What if it were *our* baby?" She uses the conditional verb correctly, even when she talks. It drives me crazy. "What if that lady had kidnapped our baby because you were negligent?"

6

Negligent or not, I like it when she hints that she likes me enough to consider having *our* baby some day. Still, I had to defend myself. "I was only looking at lettuce. You want me to grab any old rotten head of lettuce for you, in case some old lady is lurking around waiting to steal our imaginary baby? You know how careful you have to be with the produce in that place."

"For the time being," she said, "you can pick out a good head of lettuce, but this is not making me trust you enough to let you take the baby out alone. You're going to have to start doing better. I won't have you handing our baby away at the market."

"Next time I'll *carry* the baby."

She rolled her eyes at me. "Right. You're going to get an 80-pound bag of dog food into the cart with one arm?"

"Eighty-pound bag of what?"

"Dog food."

"For what?"

"Duh! For Barney."

"No. We are not naming the baby Barney." I didn't even get into how wrong it would be to make him eat dog food.

"Don't be an idiot. The baby's name is Wendell Enrique. Barney's our mastiff."

She can go on and on like that without ever cracking a smile.

It wasn't such a joke when it happened, though. What kind of world do we live in, where shopping cart wrestlers roam the produce section? I marched right after that lady. I made it about three steps too. Then I imagined catching up to her. In my imagination, she was a fighter. We got in a fierce tug-of-war over the cart, which had to be broken up by a combination of store employees and nearby customers. In all the possible alternate endings I could visualize, I never got to be the innocent victim. Every time, she was an upstanding, middle-aged lady, and I was a young thug. I learned a lesson in those three steps, which I will

7

share with you. If you are a man in your twenties, you might be able to win a shopping cart tug-of-war with a lady in her forties or fifties, but it will be a Pyrrhic victory. No matter whose cart it was to begin with, you won't be able to shop in that store again. In these modern times, wars are won in hearts and minds, and a middle-aged lady in a grocery store is a propaganda machine.

Beaten by her sneak attack, I retreated to the front of the store to get a new cart. There were none left. Through the front windows I could see carts strewn about the parking lot. I retreated further to get one of these, but by the time I got outside, I was broken. Halfway to the first cart, I stopped and glanced back at the storefront. What I saw was an insane asylum. I walked past the cart to my car.

Had we been in desperate need of eggs or something, I'm sure I would have strapped my courage into the toddler seat and marched right back in there with a new cart. I would have held onto it tightly and probably punched anybody who came within two feet of it. I would have stood up and done my marketing like a man. But we didn't need anything all that badly, so I tucked my tail and limped home.

Gwen went later and did our shopping. She didn't get any carts swiped. It wasn't because there weren't old ladies lurking around, just waiting for the chance to strike. No, it was because Gwen is all set up to be a responsible parent. She made sure to point out that distinction to me.

2.
Marge Meko: Temp Killer

The most important thing to know about being a temp at Downslope College is: keep your mouth shut. There's not as much accountability at Downslope as there could be. If you come from a culture where there is more accountability—where, for example, wasting thousands of dollars is frowned upon—you might be tempted to point out something that you ought not point out. You have to learn not to notice too many errors, because fixing errors is oftentimes more difficult than sweeping them under the rug. Nobody wants their job to be more difficult than it needs to be, especially when they consider how easy it would be just to get rid of a meddlesome temp.

During my second week on the job, I was assigned the task of filing some paid invoices. Within a few minutes, it became clear that many of the invoices were duplicates. Marge Meko, the payables clerk, had paid them twice. What puzzled me was that the accounting program we use won't let you pay an invoice number to the same vendor more than once. Later, I discovered that Marge makes up random invoice numbers when she's inputting the billing information. It's too much trouble to lean forward and read the real number off the invoice.

I stewed over my discovery. I didn't want to get Marge Meko in trouble. I was a temp, two weeks at the assignment. On the other hand, the mistakes I had seen amounted to more than $8,000. Who knew how long Marge had been overpaying? I figured people would want to know if the college were bleeding money. I decided I had to say something. This is when I learned the first real accounting rule: shut up!

I took a couple of examples to show Steve, the accounting manager. Steve was not happy to hear what I had to say. He seemed to be taking it in stride that money was being wasted. What really had him upset was that somebody was pointing out the details of the wastage to him. It soon became clear that bringing this sort of thing to him was a big mistake.

Here's what I learned from my big mistake. Steve has always assumed that money is being wasted. I think he believes that college money was born to be wasted. Further, I'm pretty sure he's been aware that the accounting department is bleeding as much or more than anybody else. He was fine with that. His boss hasn't made an issue of it. The auditors haven't seemed to notice. Everything was fine. Everybody happily looked the other way and went on living a worry-free life. Then, one day, some punk-ass kid strolls into his office with a handful of mistakes that should have been filed away and forgotten. That punk-ass kid was me, and walking into his office was my mistake.

Steve was not pleased to learn that I had fingered Marge Meko as the source of the errors. The look on his face said that Marge Meko had the goods on him. Her boat was not to be rocked. The fear in his eyes turned to anger. He was not angry with Marge Meko; he was angry with me. He was going to teach me a lesson. "Here's what I want you to do," he said. "I want you to get all that money back. Figure out where it went and get it back, every penny. Understand?"

"Wouldn't it be better if Marge did that?" It wasn't that it would be such a hard job. It would take some time, some phone calls and emails I could live without, but it wouldn't be difficult. I just didn't like being punished for somebody else's mistakes. Besides, maybe it would teach Marge Meko to take the extra second and look for the real invoice number.

"No," he said with satisfaction in his voice. "It would be better if *you* did it. You're new. It will help you understand how the process works around here." He didn't mean the process of getting back extra money paid to vendors. There was no process for getting overpayments back from vendors. The process he was speaking of was the one where you stayed away from the boss's office and kept your concerns under your desk.

"What about Marge Meko?" I asked, pushing my luck.

I expected him to be short with me; instead he was pensive. "Good point. What about Marge Meko?" He scratched his face. "Have you spoken to her about this?"

"No."

"Good. Don't." The way he said it made me sure that he wasn't planning on speaking to her either.

"She'll go on making the same mistakes," I told him.

"Okay?" he said, waiting for me to say something with a point to it. Then his face changed. "You're right. We probably can't have her making more of these mistakes . . . *now that we know about them*." He spit the last part out at me as an accusation.

He wrenched his face to indicate that he was thinking hard about the matter of Marge Meko. I started to get up from the chair I was sitting in.

"Where are you going?" he asked.

"I was leaving," I answered. "I thought you were thinking about what you were going to say to Marge Meko, and I didn't want to have my nose in things that are none of my business."

"None of your business? Like hell, it's none of your business. It's all of your business." He straightened himself up, like a man who had just made a decision. "I want you to confront her on it," he said.

"Excuse me?"

"I want you to tell Marge Meko that you've discovered her mistakes, and I want you to make her stop making them."

11

"Me? I'm a temp. Marge Meko isn't going to listen to me. You're the only one . . ."

He cut me off. "Oh no! I'm not getting dragged into this. You hear me? I forbid you to even mention my name to Marge Meko. This is just between you and her. As far as she's concerned, I don't know anything about it."

"How can I make her change?" I protested. "I'm not her boss. I'm not even her peer."

"I don't know. And I don't care. Just fix the problem you've made, and then forget it ever happened. I don't want to hear another word about it. Now go." He pointed toward the door with such violence that I expected to hear a shoulder tendon pop.

I got up. "Gray," he called after me. "I mean it. I don't want to hear another word about this—from anybody."

I didn't approach Marge Meko that day. I needed a night to lie in bed and contemplate how I would manage the confrontation. When I finally got to sleep, I was assailed by nightmares in which I was assaulted by Marge Meko, in the guises of: a professional wrestler, the shadowy proprietress of the house of wax, and, I think, Hitler. In the morning, Gwen wanted to know who Marge Meko was, because I had shouted out her name in my sleep. Gwen probably would have been more upset about it, except that I didn't seem to be enjoying whatever it was that this mysterious Marge Meko was doing to me. Gwen was right; my neck was still sore from the headlock.

I resolved to get the monkey off my back first thing in the morning. I determined that I would be as diplomatic with Marge Meko as I could possibly manage. Since I had no power to compel her to change her work practices, there was no point in antagonizing her.

At quarter after eight I pulled a chair to the side of her desk and sat down. "Can I talk to you for a minute, Marge?" I said softly.

"Who are you?" she asked. "And how do you know my name?"

If I may give a few words of description, Marge Meko is a stout, fifty-something woman. She has curly, brown hair that sits atop her head in resemblance to a Chia Pet. She has frighteningly thick arms with pudgy little hands, which she balls up into compact fists when she is agitated. She is not an exceptionally bright person, but she is just smart enough to be dangerous. She knows what she needs to know to keep her job, and how to keep it cushy. She knows little about how to do her job properly, and she doesn't care to know. She has learned that doing her job properly is not necessary, and may even be harmful, when it comes to maintaining the good life. She's been around for a long time because she has sharp animal instincts, and leaves no doubt that if she's ever made to go, she's taking a few people with her. She gets good merit raises every year, and takes time off when she wants it. Her superiors have decided that those concessions are a small price to pay to stay on her good side. She can't multiply six times three without using a calculator, but in the world of college politics, she's a very smart employee.

"I'm Gary Gray." I swallowed hard. "I've been temping here for almost two weeks."

She scrutinized my face. "Yeah, I've seen you around. I thought you were the kid who delivered the bottles for the water cooler."

"Actually, I've been filing your paid invoices."

"Oh, have you now?" She was very quiet and calm, yet there was something ominous behind the tranquility.

"Yeah, and Marge, I've found something that I thought you would want to know about."

Her eyebrows arched. She'd been playing the game too long to miss the alert, despite my lame diplomacy. Her little hands began forming into fists. "Oh indeed, Mr. Gray. I'm very curious

13

to know what it is you think you've found among my invoices after nearly two whole weeks mastering the ropes of this department. By all means, do tell."

"Well, Ms. Meko," I didn't feel confident calling her Marge anymore. "It looks like some of the invoices might have been paid more than once."

"And how, after two weeks, excuse me, *nearly* two weeks, of temporary filing duty, did you come to that conclusion?"

Fortunately, I had thought to bring an example with me. I showed her two copies, each with a payment stub stapled to the front. The stubs indicated that a check for $403.38 had been issued for each copy. Marge Meko examined the evidence long enough to see that it proved my assertion before tossing the papers back at me. "Did Steve put you up to this?" she demanded, squinting daggers toward the accounting manager's office.

"No, absolutely not," I lied. "He doesn't know anything about it. I didn't see any need to get him involved. I just thought you would want to know about this. I mean, if the roles were reversed, I absolutely would want you to tell me."

She didn't believe me. "You sure you didn't go running straight to him with these invoices to show off how clever a little temp you are? You sure he didn't send you out here cause he's too chickenshit to face me?"

My face must have been beet red. "No, no. This is just between you and me." Sensing that I was too eager in my defense, I tried the casual tact. "You know, I just thought I'd give you the heads up, in case you wanted to know. But hey, just say the word, and I'll keep these things to myself when they happen . . ." Marge Meko's left eye began to twitch. "I mean, *if* they happen . . ." That didn't ease the twitch. "I mean, you know, I'll keep things to myself."

"Oh, I've got a word for you: stop trying to blame *your* incompetence on *me*."

14

"What?"

"Don't play dumb with me, temp. I see what's going on here. You were supposed to file away these invoices, and you didn't know how to do it. Or maybe you were just too lazy to do it. Was that it? Too lazy? Too lazy to find a real job? Too lazy to file a few invoices away? Huh? I bet they call you 'Lazy Temp Gary Gray', don't they?" The name did have a certain ring to it, and she was on to something about me being lazy. I certainly am too lazy, for example, to process payment twice on the same invoice. So I let her go on without interrupting, to see if she had additional reasonable points to make. "Instead of filing those invoices, like you were told, you just threw the whole pile back in my basket. Figured nobody would notice, didn't you? Well, I guess you ran up against somebody just a little bit smarter than you."

"Who?" I asked.

"Don't screw with me, temp boy. Your crap don't fly here." She pushed her chair back from her desk. I thought she was about to put me into a headlock and make me say "Uncle" like in my dream. Instead, she swiveled herself around so that we were eye to eye. "This is what's going to happen now," she commanded. "You are going to go back to whatever hole you crawled out of and keep quiet. I don't care if you do your job or not; I'm not your babysitter. But, you are not ever going to blame your problems on me again. Next time you try something like that, we'll see what Steve has to say about it. I should let him know what you're up to right now, but I'm too soft-hearted. Now, get away from me, before I change my mind."

I'd told Steve that there was no point in sending me to talk to Marge Meko, hadn't I? Yes, I believe I had. But then, when you realize that Steve wasn't looking for results, so much as he was looking for excuses, I guess it was as good a management decision as any he's made.

For a couple days I actually worried that Marge Meko

would go on making her mistakes, and Steve would hold me accountable for failing to change her ways. I needn't have worried. It wasn't that Marge Meko changed her ways; she went on double-paying invoices. She was a little more careful about it for a few days before she slipped right back into her old habits. Yet, Steve seemed to have forgotten about the issue altogether. I guess when he said he wanted to hear no more about it, that's exactly what he meant. At least he's a man of his word.

The only thing Steve mentioned that touched upon the matter came a couple of weeks later. I had collected refund checks from the overpaid vendors, in strict accordance with the punishment for my gratuitous whistle blowing. I'd gotten about $4,000 back, and was expecting more any day. When Steve called me into his office, I thought he was going to give me grief for not having gotten more of it back already. That just proves how slow on the up-take I am.

"I see you've turned in quite a few refund checks," Steve said. It didn't sound like he was displeased with only $4,000.

"Yeah, there should be more coming next week."

His eyes fell down to the floor. "How many more?"

"Three or four checks, another grand maybe."

He sighed. "You should be doing collections. Seems like you're pretty good at this." His tone was not complimentary.

"It's not that hard," I said. "Our vendors don't want random payments sitting around on their books. Most are eager to give it back."

"Listen Gary, maybe it's time for you to take a break from pursuing this money. I mean, all these checks coming in, it's out of the ordinary. People aren't always comfortable with things that are out of the ordinary. Besides, I think you've learned your lesson."

I'd learned a lot of lessons in those few weeks. One of them was that people aren't always comfortable with things that are out of the ordinary because things that are out of the ordinary often cause outsiders to look more closely at the ordinary, and people who have been turning a blind eye toward the ordinary don't often want outsiders to examine it closely. There's nothing like things that are out of the ordinary to raise red flags; Steve was decidedly opposed to red flags being raised up over the accounting department.

"There's still $3,000 out there that I could get back— and that's just the money I know about," I protested. I didn't say it out of naiveté. I knew damned well that Steve didn't care about that money. I guess I wanted to pretend to be naive, just to force Steve to admit that he didn't care.

"Oh, well, let's not be too greedy, okay?" That was a ridiculous thing to say. It was our money, after all. But, it was as close as I could bring him to confessing that responsibly stewarding the college's assets was the least of his concerns.

After the next week, no more refund checks came. Steve was very pleased with my decreased productivity. Had I not been a temp, I'm sure I would have made Employee of the Month.

3.

Cavemen Could Just Spread Their Seed, and Not Worry About Diamond Rings

The whole incident where I lost our imaginary baby in the grocery store seems to have flipped some kind of switch within Gwen. Ever since, she has been making noises about her biological clock ticking. She's 24, for Pete's sake! The sun hasn't even fully risen on her biological day. I suspect she's somehow put herself on Greenwich Mean Time, because she's gotten five or six hours ahead of herself. I just need to find a way to turn the hour hand back to where it should be without her noticing. Good luck to me, right?

Sometimes I think she just wants to get back onto the family Christmas card. Her parents have a family portrait taken every October to put on the front of their Christmas cards. At first, it included Gwen, her parents, her brother, Dale, and Rex, their German Wirehaired Pointer. When Dale got married, his wife, Georgia, joined the group. Then, Gwen moved in with me. I guess she didn't figure the family portrait into that calculation. Gwen was okay with having her parents cut her off financially, but the portrait imbroglio hit her hard. She had picked out a nice Christmasy sweater for me to wear and everything. Then, the word came down. Of course, she could be in the picture. Her parents still loved her, in spite of her unfortunate choices. But I was out, no ifs ands or buts. I was not family, and my presence on the card would only reinforce to all of their kith and kin that their daughter was living in sin.

I tried to convince Gwen to go sit for the portrait. It was no big deal, I told her. I'd not been on Christmas cards all of my life, and another year of not reaching that milestone wouldn't kill me. But my Gwen is a fighter. I was her guy, so she took it as an insult that her parents didn't want me blemishing their spotless tableau. If they didn't take me, they wouldn't get her. It turned out that her parents are fighters too. So now Gwen has missed three Christmas cards. I'm not sure how her parents explain their disappeared daughter to family and friends (she's a lot like Chuck on *Happy Days*), but I guess they get by, whatever their story is. Now it's just Mom, Dad, Dale, Georgia, and Rex. Incidentally, it's common knowledge that Rex did impregnate the Collie down the street two years ago, but he had the good sense not to move in with her, so he is not living in sin. Presumably, that is the difference between himself and Gwen.

Don't tell Gwen this, but I'm actually a little relieved that I'm not invited to be on her family's Christmas card. I have nothing against her family, in spite of my uncertain status in their view of reality, but I'm not sure I'm ready to hand over the rights to my likeness to them. I've got my own family after all. It's not that my folks have ever put a family portrait on a Christmas card, or ever will. As a unit, we're not nearly as photogenic as Gwen's family. My parents recognized the folly of mass mailing our portrait early on. Accordingly, they buy the cheapest Christmas cards they can find and soothe our familial homeliness with big savings. Nonetheless, I can't help but wonder what their reaction to seeing me on another family's Christmas card would be. It would be like saying that I had become dissatisfied with the lack of publicity I had been receiving from my own family, and had quit them and signed up with a new group who were willing to offer me a little face time.

Imagine seeing your kid suddenly show up in somebody

else's family portrait. Then, imagine that portrait showing up in your mailbox with supposed good tidings attached to it. That'd be a real kick in the teeth, wouldn't it? I can just see my parents getting that card. My mom shows my dad: "Look, Hal, we got another portrait card from the Goldblatts."

Dad takes the card and looks it over. "Damn, that family is handsome! Another year older though. Don't worry, it'll catch up to them one day."

My mom says, "Yeah, something's different though. The picture seems more cluttered than usual."

Dad says, "You're right. Hey, I think they got a new kid. He's not so cute as the rest. Looks familiar."

Mom says, "No, he's not much of a looker at all, is he?"

"Well I'll be a son of a bitch!" dad blurts out. "That's Gary!"

"Let me see." Mom takes the card back. "You know, I think you're right." She sniffles. "He *seemed* happy with us. Why would he have taken up with another family?"

Dad gets stern. "I don't know, and I don't care. If that's the way he wants it, fine. We don't need him; we've got those others."

Dad puts an arm around Mom and pulls her close. Through her tears, Mom says, "Look, the girl came back too. I wonder where she's been, these past years."

Dad takes another look. "Yup, she's back all right. Now *she's* a looker."

In reality, my parents would get over my being on the Goldblatt family Christmas card a lot quicker than Gwen will get over my not being on the card. The reasons why she's so sensitive about the card issue go far beyond the card itself. She wants her parents' respect and approval. While all I've got to do to keep my parents' approval is avoid ditching them for a better position in a new family, Gwen's parents have this crazy idea that children should *earn* their parents' approval. Rule number one in Mama

20

and Papa Goldblatt's Big Book of Approval Credits and Debits is that you marry someone before you go in halfsies on a queen-size bed with them.

Gwen broke rule number one, and lost big points, which may be part of the reason why she is warming to the idea of marriage. She might be able to win some of those points back by doing the right thing, even if it's in the wrong order. Or maybe, in spite of it all, she wouldn't mind so much being married to me. I guess I should look at it that way and be happy about the direction things are going, because, for one thing, my dad is right, she is a looker. On top of that, her reading comprehension skills are incredible. Someone with that combination has no business hitching her biological clock to a wagon like mine. I should probably just go along and let her chain herself to me before she wakes up, because for her there will be a lot of other fish in the sea—eager and willing fish. Then there's me. I'm like the little row-boat fisherman who pulled in a fish that everybody thought was extinct for a million years. If I'm dumb enough to throw that one back, I might as well swear off fishing, because I'm never going to hit a jackpot like that again.

On the other hand, I can't help equating marriage to some sort of commitment. There's nothing wrong with commitments, as long as you can get out of them easily enough. But marriage is a biggie. I know it makes no sense for a guy who's lucked into the best woman he could ever hope for to want to keep his options open, but does a man's prerogative to flee need to make sense? I say, don't question your God-given rights. Okay, here it is, the next breath, and I'm already questioning them. I have to. I mean, I could never get another girl as bright or as attractive as Gwen, let alone the combination of the two. Yet I have this instinct to leave the door open to possibilities. So what am I doing? I'm holding out for the chance to snag a dumber, plainer girl. Great, that's just what I need to be doing. Seriously, I know I'm not a super hero, but my self-esteem isn't that low either. I really don't need to be involved in this tag line: "World's Stupidest Fisherman Splits with Prehistoric Fish."

Fear is not very reasonable, is it? I'm afraid to commit to the best girl I could ever find, with whom I am perfectly happy. And why am I afraid? Well, as best I can figure, it boils down to my subconscious, caveman desire to pass around my genetic code. Now this is truly ridiculous. There's no one on earth I would rather marry than Gwen. But if I do so, I lose some sort of moral right to spread my seed among the various women I see who are attractive to me. Of course, no man, in today's world, could afford to spread his seed in this manner. In fact, men who pursue attractive women for sexual purposes generally take positive steps to prohibit their seed from taking root among their far-flung conquests. This so-called biological imperative has overstayed its welcome among humanity, and yet we can't quite kick it out the door.

What makes matters even more ridiculous is that even if I retained my freedom to have one-night-stands all over the place, I would never use it. I've never had a one-night-stand, and I've never wanted to have one. If I lived back in caveman days, and didn't have to worry about AIDS or herpes, I'd probably be a one-night-stand carnival. Yeah, you know, I like boobies. I think they're great. And they're just one part of the stuff that's good. But I'm not into Russian Roulette. I really can get what I need out of one, good, clean set of boobies, and etcetera. And the crazy thing is that I've got exactly that, bedding down next to me every night.

This fear of commitment just gets stupider and stupider. I'm making progress against it though. I even let Gwen drag me into jewelry stores every once in a while. Gwen is not a particularly materialistic woman. Sure, she likes to look good, but she knows the value of a dollar (the few we have, and the many we don't), and she's got enough creativity to dive into a clearance rack and come out with something she can use. Still, the fact that cannot be denied is that Gwen has a weakness for shiny things. Most jewelry and assorted baubles, Gwen could easily ignore. But when it comes to diamonds, I have trouble telling if that sparkle is coming from the stones or Gwen's eyes.

Gwen looks at diamond rings with an absolute girlish delight. I guess that's why I let her drag me into the jewelry stores at all. She's so cute and innocent when she looks at diamond rings. I can just about see all her little girl dreams of her fairy tale wedding dance across her eyes. I can understand how you might think that I'm kidding myself and rationalizing away my lady's flashes of materialism by painting her as a day-dreaming 10-year-old. Maybe I am doing just that, but what strikes me about Gwen and diamonds is that she has the same glow about her regardless of the size and price of the diamond. The sales people can try to talk her up toward the high end all they want, but it doesn't seem to matter. Gwen can see her childhood Prince Charming in them all—within reason. She has to be able to see the diamond after all, because I'm sure she never dreamt that Prince Charming would sweep her away to his mobile home.

Even though she can work herself into giddiness over modest diamonds, she has developed a list of her favorite characteristics. How could she be a respectable woman if she had not? She points out different things to me, just so I'll have an idea of what she prefers, should the day ever come when I choose to make an honest woman out of her. I guess that's a good thing, because I can see that happening—some day—and I'm sure I will need all the help I can get to cut through the confusion.

The confusion will be great. No matter how many times a salesperson goes over the differences in cut and clarity with us, I always find myself trying to compare two relatively shiny rocks. I confess: to me, that's what they are. The bigger shiny rock costs more than the smaller shiny rock, right? Then, they have you look at them through that magnifying glass. Guess what? They're still shiny rocks. But this one costs three times more than that one. Go figure! Oh, this one has three more facets? Great! Those extra facets will come in handy when we're living out of our car.

One time I decided that I was going to bear down and really try to learn how the whole diamond game worked. No fooling around; I was serious. The store had this event where a special representative brought in a bunch of loose diamonds that people could put into whatever setting they like. Each diamond had a little card with it that showed all the specifications: price, size, color, cut, clarity, and a bunch of angle measurements and ratios. There were some diamonds that looked pretty similar. According to their cards, the specifications were pretty close, but the prices were wildly different. I picked out an example of this. "Why is this diamond so much more expensive than that one?" I asked. "They seem pretty much the same."

"Oh no," the special representative said. "This one is a superior cut." She pointed to the more expensive one.

"But the cut is described the same on both cards," I protested. "It almost seems that these diamonds are priced randomly, but I know that can't be true." Actually, I did not know at all that it couldn't be true. In fact, from all of the confusing and conflicting lessons I had suffered through, I was becoming more and more convinced that diamonds were indeed priced by the luck of the draw.

"Let me show you the difference," she said. Then she went into a long explanation about ratios. I felt like I was able to follow her explanation, except for the part that seemed like she made up on the spot. When she was done, I got out a pen and paper and started making comparative notes about various diamonds. Then I started doing some math using various numbers I had written down from the diamond cards. "What are you doing?" she asked with a politeness that belied her growing annoyance with my insistence on questioning the system.

"I'm trying to figure out how diamonds are priced. There must be a formula or something."

Even if there were a formula, or for that matter, any fundamental rhyme or reason, to the way diamonds are priced, I was not going to come anywhere close to finding it, doing basic algebra there at the counter. Even so, she did not appreciate my attempt to pry into these matters. "Oh, it's all far more complicated than that," she told me, without trying to hide her distaste for my line of inquiry. She began putting the diamonds she had taken out for us back into the case without asking if we were done looking at them. "There are all kinds of other factors involved."

"For example?" I asked. I was thinking that one of the primary 'other factors' might be how far behind her sales plan she was for the month, but I didn't volunteer that idea.

"It'd be too complicated to get into right now. Besides I have other customers waiting." She closed and locked the case in front of us. Without another word she sidled a couple feet to her right and said a pleasant hello to a couple that was gazing into the glass down there.

The lesson I took away was that there is a very specific reason why each diamond costs what it does, but nobody knows what the reason is. I suppose that if I wanted to make huge profits selling diamonds, I would set them at wide variations in price. That way the people who want a bargain would buy the cheaper ones, and the people who believe that what's twice as expensive is twice as good would buy the expensive ones. If all like diamonds were priced alike, probably no one would buy any of them. You couldn't brag about the bargain you got, or that price is no object; and those are the two best reasons for buying shiny bits of stone, aren't they?

One peculiar phenomenon I have noticed in our visits to jewelry stores is the difference in sales techniques between the men and the women who work in those places. There are some exceptions, but overall, the men seemed much more chatty than the women. The men sought to beguile us with friendly conversation, while the women just wanted to know if we were really going to buy anything, as opposed to wasting their time asking innumerable questions, the answers to which we would not understand anyway.

The male salesman would ask your name. He would then proceed to address you by name every time he said something. He would ask a lot of personal things that had nothing to do with diamonds, like, "How long have you been dating, Gary? Are you originally from this area, Gwen? Oh? Where are you from, Gwen?" Having extracted such personal information from you, he would expound on the coincidental likenesses between your life story and his own. Anything you could say was certainly familiar to him. You could tell him you were from the south pole and he would tie it back to his experiences. "It's beautiful country down there, isn't it? I'm from down that way myself. Texas. I didn't get a chance to go down any further toward the south pole, but I would have liked to. It's pretty much the same neighborhood, anyway." Here's where he would chuckle a little bit. "They got a lot of those penguins down your way, don't they? Yeah, I like penguins, always make a point to go look at them when we're at the zoo. Those little guys are great, aren't they?" Then he might go into something about polar bears. If you told him that there weren't any polar bears within a hemisphere and a half of the south pole, he'd just laugh it off. "Oh, that's right. I just had a couple in here from the north pole. That's why I'm confused."

During the next half hour of storytelling, you might sneak in a few questions about diamonds, but more likely, you'd have lost all interest in jewels. Your top priority would be breaking away from the guy in a socially acceptable manner, as if he were your lonely old great-grandpa at the nursing home. The long goodbye would be awkward. You'd leave him with that innocent faith in his eyes that you'd be back, because how could you buy a ring from anybody but the guy who was practically your brother? You'd also be worried that he was likely to show up at your house for dinner one night. You'd spend the next hour racking your brain to remember if he had weaseled your home address out of you.

The women jewelers I have met on my whirlwind tour seem far less interested in getting invited to our place for dinner. They don't want to be friends with me. Maybe diamonds mean more to women, and that makes it harder to be friends with the people who are snatching them up from right under your nose. I mean, if I worked in a sports collectibles store, and people kept coming in, toying with my emotions by acting like they were going to buy the Joe Montana autographed football that I could not afford, I wouldn't want to be their friend either. I don't know, maybe it's nothing like that at all. All I can say is: if I have to hand over to you, to take home and enjoy, the autographed football that I've been drooling over for years, you are nothing but a bastard to me and I never want to be your friend. I only hope that I'm working on commission so I can get a little chunk of your money.

Maybe that has nothing to do with why the women were more business-like, but they definitely were more business-like. One lady was showing us a few different rings, without much small talk, which was fine with me. I noticed that there was one ring that Gwen seemed to really like. I looked at the price on the tag and asked the lady if it were negotiable. She gave me one of those vague answers, like: "We might be able to go a little lower on this piece." Then she went on to muddy the waters even more with some drivel about it being one of their signature diamonds, and how they couldn't be as flexible with signature diamonds as they would like.

I hate receiving vague answers, the fact that I often give them notwithstanding. The lady annoyed me into getting very specific with her, even though I was not nearly ready to get very specific about any particular ring in the world. "What is the best price you could give on that ring?" I asked.

She frowned as if my question had been an affront to her character. Then, she went all used car salesman on me. "If I go ask him," she tossed a glance over her shoulder toward some mythical "him" at the back of the store (the God of diamond ring prices, presumably), "for that price, he's going to want to know, 'Are they buying today?'" She looked down at me, like she had me backed into the very spot where she wanted me. "What shall I tell him?"

If I had wanted to hear a question like that, I'd be down at the "Bad Credit, No Problem!" lot, eyeing a 1994 Buick. I must have been getting angry, because Gwen told me later that I responded in a very soft, measured tone. "You can tell him this," I said. "Very soon we will be buying a diamond ring. In the meantime, we are collecting all the relevant information we can about the rings we like from various jewelry stores. If there is anything that you, or he, want to tell us that might persuade us to choose this ring, I invite you to tell us now."

I can bet she wanted to tell us to go jump in the lake, but she did need to make a living, so she reluctantly went off to consult with the all-powerful "him." A minute later she came back with the manager of the store. He was a man, so rather than speak of such a cold thing as the price of diamond rings, he made nice introductions and asked us where we were from. In the next thirty minutes we learned quite a bit about his youthful exploits, back in our neck of the woods. We didn't learn anything about how much money he would take for the ring Gwen liked. Finally, we made disingenuous promises about coming back to visit him again some time, so we could go home and rest. Gwen said she actually felt kind of bad leading that man to believe that we might actually buy a ring from his store. I think she got over the guilt pretty quickly though, because as soon as we got home she curled up on the couch and went to sleep. When you feel more sleepy than guilty, I suspect your conscience will be okay.

I don't mean to leave the impression that Gwen drags me into a different jewelry store every weekend. First of all, she doesn't actually drag me; I go because I know it's something she enjoys, and as long as I can keep her happy just looking at rings, well, hey, bonus. Second, we don't go all that often. Sure, Gwen likes to look at all the rings, but she knows what I'll be able to afford. I know she'll graciously accept what little I can give her and never complain. So why should I care if she wants to daydream a little in the meantime? She's really a very practical woman, so I like it that she allows herself to daydream once in a while. It seems quite natural that she should daydream about her wedding. She's been doing that since she was about five years old. In fact, it took her by surprise to learn that I did not daydream about such things. I had to explain to her that it wasn't really the typical thing for men to daydream about. No little boy who grew up to marry a woman, I explained, has ever daydreamed about his wedding. When she wanted to know what men *did* daydream about, I changed the subject.

I'm a little afraid now that you might think Gwen just wants to get married so that she can climb back onto the Christmas card with her family. If you think that, it's my fault for not representing things properly. Yes, it hurt Gwen to get kicked off the Christmas card, and she would dearly love to get back on it. No doubt, it means a lot to her. But that just shows how much she's sacrificed for me. I almost wish my parents would give me some ultimatum that I could defy for the sake of my love for Gwen, just to show that I would make the same sacrifices for her. The problem is that my parents aren't the disowning type. The fact is, they never really laid claim to me in the first place. It's not that they don't love me. I mean, there had to be something behind those eighteen years of free room and board. It's only that we all just do our own thing. Whereas Gwen's parents maintain the right (and even the responsibility) to impose sanctions if their kid goes astray of their value system, my parents' only firm belief about their adult children is that visiting them in jail is purely voluntary.

If I get nothing else across, understand this: I am a very lucky man to have a woman like Gwen wanting to marry me and, presumably, have my children. I know that she wants to have children, so I'm assuming, based on the evidence at hand, that she expects them to be mine. This brings up another potential issue: how can I give the baby enough DNA to make it whole, but little enough that it looks 100 percent like Gwen? I have this nightmare where someone comments that our newborn child has my nose, or chin, or ears, and Gwen just bursts into tears. How's that for postpartum depression? I guess she'll have to count on the strength of a mother's love to get her over it. I'll certainly sympathize with her, but the bottom line is: she made her bed, she'll just have to lie in it—possibly with an infant, who looks way too much like me, cuddled up in her arms.

4.

In His Idiocy's Secret Service

Just when I think the whole Marge Meko incident is put behind me, Steve calls me into his office. Steve is a man with a lot of secrets. I guess that would tend to drive a person toward paranoia after a while. I think it also leads to a tendency to beat around the bush, rather than come out with what's on your paranoid mind. A man as paranoid as Steve will start beating his way around the bush, leaving himself no less than a good 30-mile radius. Hence, it can take a while to understand why Steve called you into his office.

When Steve circled to within about 10 miles of the bush, I understood that he had been thinking about Marge Meko, and her mistakes. When he got to within about five miles of the bush, I realized that Steve had been obsessing about Marge Meko, and her mistakes. Marge Meko had likely been making the same mistakes for many years. A non-paranoid manager might have been comforted by the fact that, in all that time, those mistakes had never come back to bite him. A paranoid manager could very easily convince himself that he had been riding a very long lucky streak—a lucky streak that was bound to end sooner or later.

Steve was clearly worried about the longevity of his lucky streak. What if he got a new boss? What if the college hired a new auditor? In general, what if someone who had the power to examine the records suddenly started to give a damn? Then he'd be screwed. I don't think he was worried about losing his job. As far as he could tell, there was no precedent at Downslope College for firing someone merely over gross incompetence and criminal neglect. He was far more worried about what his job would become. People might expect him to keep track of his employees, and check on their work. Somebody might actually expect him to notice the output of his department. Steve doesn't know much about those aspects of management, but he does know that they smell like hard work, and what would be the point of having a job like that? That wasn't what he went to school for.

Steve had come to the uncomfortable conclusion that it would be best to put a stop to Marge Meko's double-paying of invoices. As hard as that was for Steve to accept, it was the easy part. The hard part was doing it without getting Marge Meko involved. Marge Meko was dangerous in so many different ways that it was quite impossible for a man like Steve to ask her to reform her work habits. She was, in fact, too dangerous for Steve to even insinuate that some of her habits might need reform. After much thought, and little ethical consideration, Steve had hit upon a different way to come at the problem. I wasn't called to his office to hear about this different way; I *was* the different way.

Marge Meko has an IN basket on the corner of her desk, where people put invoices that need paying. In theory, Marge enters the invoice information into the accounting software on her computer, cuts a check, and files a copy of the paid invoice in a place where it will be clear that said invoice has been paid. Marge Meko is not much for filing. She is not much for putting anything where it belongs. Most of the paid invoices eventually find their way to the paid invoice file; meanwhile, many of them get strewn around the building so wildly that a good portion find their way, at the hand of some helpful Samaritan, back to Marge Meko's IN basket. That might not become a problem, except that Marge Meko does not discriminate; she distrusts all co-workers, and she pays all invoices. Still, there needn't be a problem, were it not for Marge Meko's habit of inventing invoice numbers, rather than

32

leaning forward far enough to read the intended number off the actual invoice. This is where Marge Meko breaks free of all safeguards that were put in place to prevent people almost like her from causing chaos in the office. No one has ever developed a safeguard for people exactly like Marge Meko, although that is just what Steve was foolishly proposing to do with an unlikely safeguard by the name of Gary Gray.

I was the chosen one, the one anointed to solve the Marge Meko problem. How was I to do it? Was I to help her devise a system that would allow her to recognize invoices that had already been paid? No. I was not to speak to her about it at all. I was to go under cover. This was a covert operation. Steve made it clear that if Marge Meko ever found me out, he would deny all knowledge of my activities. It would, after all, be rather unseemly for a manger to be involved in such behind-the-back operations against one of his employees.

Come in early, stay late, loiter around the office at lunchtime—the time of my skulking was up to me. At whatever time I chose, provided Marge Meko was out of sight, I was to rifle through her IN box, placing a small, discrete mark on each of the invoices. As if I could not figure out all the complexities of his plan for myself, Steve stressed that this mark must be inconspicuous to Marge Meko but easily recognizable to myself. At least once a day I was to repeat my raid upon Marge Meko's IN box, weeding out the invoices that already had my mark on them, and marking the others. The invoices I culled from the pile, I was to file in the appropriate place for paid invoices, so that they would never again find their way into the vicious circle. That was it. That was the ingenious plan resulting from all the hours of Steve's obsessive brooding. "So simple that it's genius," was the way he described it. "So stupid that it's asinine," was the phrase that occurred to me. I might have pointed out (though it would have done no good) that training Marge Meko to place a simple mark on the invoices as she paid them—say, something as complicated as a check mark—would have accomplished the same end without most of the trouble and any of the skullduggery. You will be proud to know that I did not waste anybody's precious time in pointing it out.

Now, I'm a professional spy. As far as Steve is concerned, that's my job. Anything else I happen to do while I'm at the office is nice, but my supervisor will take no note of it. To him, my sole purpose for being employed is to snoop through Marge Meko's IN basket. Just call me double-0 . . . what number should come after that? Probably another 0. That's about what I feel my contribution has been limited to. Agent 00-0, at your service—triple-0, for short. I have seven levels to go up before I get my license to kill. At triple-0 status, you only get a license to pilfer redundant paperwork from incompetent data coders. Not too shabby for a temp though. Right now I'm torn between working my way to a license to kill, or company-paid health insurance. I could see either one of them coming in handy, so it's a tough call.

I guess I shouldn't complain. After all, I'm adding to my skills set in ways I never imagined. How many people get to practice sneak-thieving on company time, with the blessing of their boss? When my assignment here is over, I'll need to find another position. If that one happens to be in organized crime, guess who's going to hit the ground running? A job in organized crime might be a welcome change too. At least it's organized.

Steve seems relieved now that he has put measures (me and my shadow) in place to minimize mistakes in the office. Did I say, "minimize mistakes?" I meant to say, "cover his ass." I'm the Secret Service of Steve's ass. I bet he fantasizes about me diving in front of his ass to take the administrative bullet that is aimed at it. I bet, in his mind, it's one of those slow motion scenes. Out of the corner of my eye, I spot the shooter: some overzealous, whistle-blower type. That's when my training kicks in. I repeat the mantra that has been drilled into my head in the Ass-Guarding Academy. "Must protect Steve's ass!" Then I dive out in front of his behind, screaming (still in slow motion), "Noooooooooo!" I take the bullet in the heart. Steve's ass resumes normal speed motion, in its usual backward direction, and continues enjoying its cushy executive chair while Steve finds a new temp to walk behind him.

I think this fantasy is behind the knowing looks Steve has begun giving me. It's like we're on the same secret team now, fighting the good fight against Marge Meko's incompetence. I wonder if there's anybody fighting against Steve's incompetence. Actually, I think his incompetence is at war with itself. For instance, I wonder what's going to happen when we save the thousands of dollars that Marge Meko would normally throw away. Is anybody going to wonder why the school is not that much over budget again this year (or if Marge Meko's mistakes have been built into the budget, why the school is that much under budget)? If Steve were on the ball, he could probably turn this to his advantage, pretend that he's been pressuring vendors for better discounts, or something. But Steve won't think of that. He'll just be terrified if anybody notices the difference. In Steve's book, to receive praise means that someone is paying attention, and all attention is bad. I imagine that if the topic of the extra money ever comes up, he'll just call me into his office and present another ingenious plan where I step in front of his ass in the nick of time.

Steve is taking the calculated risk that he will grow old and die before he is hauled off to jail. On the other hand, I don't know that Steve is doing anything blatantly illegal; all I have uncovered so far is just the willful negligence. I'm not sure if he could be hauled off to jail for that or not. It's probably not worth the trouble to the authorities. I mean, prosecuting people who are wasting the public's money would be too much like shooting fish in a barrel. There really wouldn't be enough sport in it to hold the attention of any police agency. I can't see it happening.

Steve's much more likely to meet his doom at the hands of Marge Meko than through the work of any fiscal investigative force. She's the one who knows how to catch him with his pants down. I have to believe she already has caught him with his pants down. She has a sixth sense for bursting into rooms where she's got no business. With all the poorly kept secrets about Steve and his many friends lingering in the air, it's hard to believe that Marge Meko hasn't hit the jackpot once.

Even so, I think Steve has less to fear from Marge Meko than he realizes. As much as he needs her to keep her mouth shut about his extracurricular doings around the school, she needs him to keep his position. It is unlikely that she could ever hold such power over a new boss. A new guy might even crack down on her work habits. She needs to keep Steve right where he is, in charge of the department, and under her thumb. That's why I don't think she'll ever really spill the beans on him. So all he has to do is keep cool and play out his bet that he will grow old and die before anybody in the world gets too interested in what happens to all the money Downslope gets from tuition and taxpayers. Really, all he has to do is keep cool; his bet is as near to a sure thing as I've ever seen.

5.

If It's a Crime to Love the Grocery Check-Out Lady, Then We Plead Guilty

Ever since the stolen cart incident, Gwen won't let me go to the store alone. She says she has to monitor my progress so she can get an idea of how long it will be before I'm responsible enough to be left alone with the baby. Also, she can see that the incident has left me a bit traumatized, and she wants to ease my anxiety. As far as I can tell, her plan is to make me feel at home in the store by making the people in the store seem like family to me. Or she could be trying to freak me out altogether just for kicks. It's too early to tell.

We were going through the check-out when Gwen decided it was Adopt a Surly Cashier Day. Whether by design or accident, we wound up in the lane of the surliest-looking cashier they had. Gwen resolved to engage the cashier in pleasant conversation, which seemed to be about the last thing the woman was interested in, or capable of. Yet, the transaction worked out okay, in that Gwen didn't get slapped or kicked. On the other hand, it wasn't any big laugh-fest or anything. In the end, Gwen came off pleased with herself, and the cashier lady was none the worse for it, as far as I could tell. She went right ahead ringing up people with that same disinterested attitude, at that same plodding pace, as she had rung up countless customers before. I'm sure she forgot all about Gwen and her pleasant conversation the moment we lugged our bags out of sight. I figured Gwen would forget about it soon enough too. I know I sure planned on forgetting about it.

The next time we were getting ready to check out with our groceries, I noticed that Gwen guided our cart into a line that was a bit longer than some of the others. When I pointed this out to her, as any sane person would do, she waved me off, as if such tactics as getting into the shortest grocery store line were not important in the big scheme of things. Now, we all know just how important finding the shortest line is, and how the horror of waiting in a line that turned out not to provide the quickest exit from the store can stick with a person and eat away at his insides. So I knew Gwen was up to something.

It didn't take long to figure out what Gwen was up to. She started chatting up the surly cashier lady as soon as the customer ahead of us had cleared the lane. Gwen dove right into friendly conversation with the woman as if they were old chums. It was evident that the cashier had no idea who Gwen was, or why she wouldn't shut up. The lady nodded and grunted monosyllable answers at Gwen just the same as I do if she starts a conversation with me when I just want to sleep. I'm not sure how badly the cashier wanted to go to sleep, but I am pretty certain that she would like to have been left alone in her little disgruntled employee world. I helped bag groceries, so that the encounter could be ended as soon as possible. Having been deprived of hours of sleep by Gwen's determined efforts at pillow talk, I felt a deep empathy for the lady. Besides that, I was not immune to the awkwardness of the situation.

The lady's demeanor lightened when the groceries were all bagged, and she had handed Gwen the receipt. I could almost see the reflection in her eyes of the light at the end of the tunnel. When Gwen assured her that we'd see her again soon, the light was snuffed right out and the lady winced. Somehow, Gwen didn't see that, because she talked all the way to the car about how nice it was to build pleasant relationships with representatives of the businesses that one frequents. On the way home, she told me how great she thought Thelma was. I had not noticed, because that's the kind of man I am, that Thelma was the name of the friendly representative of the local business with whom we had just been building a pleasant relationship.

I love Gwen dearly; she has tons of wonderful traits. But at that moment, I felt a profound sorrow for Thelma, because once Gwen decides to build a pleasant relationship with you, there's not much you can do about it. Moreover, you will have little say in the timing of the relationship building. Gwen will build it up all around you, at the time of her choosing, no matter how badly you just want to get some sleep, or be left alone to silently wallow in your hatred for your job.

Nowadays, our trips to the grocery store all begin in one of two ways. If Gwen sees Thelma working when we go in, she grabs my arm and excitedly whispers, "There's Thelma!" as if she had just caught sight of Brad Pitt. I don't know whether I should be concerned, or merely baffled, by this strange crush my girlfriend has developed on this frumpy, always-scowling woman. I know I am baffled, but should I be concerned?

If Thelma is not in sight when we enter the grocery store, Gwen gets a lost look on her face and scouts around frantically for her. "Where's Thelma?" she asks me, as if it had been my turn to babysit. Sometimes, she'll even ask the other workers if they know where Thelma is. The workers never know where Thelma is. Sometimes they don't know *who* Thelma is. This only reinforces my theory that Thelma is not the life of the party at the store's Fourth of July Employee Picnic. Clearly, Thelma does not have a lot of people watching her back among her co-workers, which makes Gwen only more nervous for her safety when she is not wedged securely between the scanner and the cash register, where she belongs.

For a long time, Thelma's eyes remained vacant with a lack of recognition every time Gwen attempted to renew their friendship. Eventually though, Gwen's image bored itself into Thelma's mind. This is an unfortunate development because vacant non-recognition represented the high point of Thelma's requital of Gwen's friendship. Now that she recognizes Gwen by sight, Thelma's eyes become expressive when they come across her, but not really in a good way. I've also noticed that when Thelma sees us come in, she often escapes the checkout area by the time we have collected our groceries. I believe that if her manager were to check, he would find that she has begun to take frequent and extended breaks. It is only a matter of time before we cause Thelma to be reprimanded, or worse.

I don't know if Thelma has discovered it yet, but the one way she can avoid having to bear our company while she scans our groceries is by working the self-serve lanes. I guess they're not really self-serve if Thelma, or some other cashier, has to work them. It would more accurate to call them mostly-self-serve lanes. There's always about one employee covering four lanes of mostly-self-serve. Perhaps mostly-self-serve is an overstatement too, because it's hard to get through there without needing that supervising employee's help on something. Usually, it's because the machine has lost track of whether or not you have placed your item in the bag. It always seems to get confused about that. Then you have to call over the live employee from where she's helping some other customer mostly-self-serve himself so that she can kick your machine, or whatever she does to make it realize that you have already put your item in the bag.

We tend to pass by the mostly-self-serve lanes. I don't like the mostly-self-serve lanes because that dumb machine never listens to me when I argue with it. Gwen doesn't like the mostly-self-serve lanes because she thinks they have caused people to lose their jobs. I don't worry about that too much because none of the homeless people I have run across make change or hand me a receipt when I give them a dollar, so I figure they're probably not out-of-work cashiers. I've tried to argue with Gwen that if every labor-saving technology that has decreased the number of workers needed had been shunned, Ford would be rolling a whopping total of three cars off its assembly lines each day. Apparently, she's not as concerned with the welfare of auto assembly workers as she is with that of grocery store cashiers. Then again, she's not as close to any auto workers as she is to Thelma. Furthermore, she has pointed out to me that she doesn't drive a Ford.

It has gotten to the point where Thelma flees the sales floor when she sees us coming. On those rare occasion when we sneak up on her before she can steal away, she has to grit her teeth and bear our pleasantness, and most likely kick herself for not being more alert. But she's our grocery store clerk and we love her.

Thelma should feel special, because there are some retail workers that we decidedly do not love. For one, there's the girl who works at the video store. We hate her. We don't know her name because we don't take the time to learn the names of the workers we hate. Well, hate is probably too strong a word, but we use it anyway. Whenever we see that we have to rent our movies from her, our first reaction is, "Ugh, I hate her!" It's become sort of a contest with us to see who can spit it out first. I usually lose, because sometimes I just want to get the movie and go home.

The reasons we hate the video store girl are a complex web of pet peeves and annoyances. This particular girl's appearance annoys you before she even opens her mouth. She looks exactly like the stereotypical precocious, twelve-year-old genius, who befuddles adults with her simple wisdom, but is socially awkward and generationally lonely, that you see on about half the dramatic series on television. Specifically, she looks like she's twelve; she has a pale, pasty complexion; she has that long, dark, curly, genius hair; she wears plastic-rimmed glasses; and she gives off a wound-up vibe, like her social isolation could cause her to snap at any minute.

These characteristics would probably not exceed the level of the mildly annoying were it not for the fact that this girl *acts* exactly like the stereotypical TV child genius. She speaks as if she's reciting from a memorized script. Moreover, she delivers her lines so furiously at you that you become convinced that she's trying to steal the scene. That would be bad enough if you were in a dramatic series, but you're in a *video store*. You're just trying to rent a movie, not remake it.

One of the reasons she seems so much like she's reciting a script is probably because she's doing just that. She's trying to sell you the crappy premium membership, and she won't take no for an answer. Now, I've worked in retail stores before where they wanted us to sell memberships to some store "rewards" program. I know that retailers spend a lot of time training the employees on what to say to make these memberships sound good. I know that they put a lot of pressure on the stores to sell their fair share of them. I also know that most of the workers understand that the reason they have their arms twisted so hard by management to push these things is that the actual rewards are usually not all that good to begin with. Furthermore, I know that most employees hate these programs and resent being forced to try to push them down the customer's throat. They say the little pre-programmed speech as often as they must to keep their jobs, and with enthusiasm in direct proportion to the rank of whatever superior might be within earshot. They take secret joy in allowing a customer to escape without having subjected him to any part of the "rewards" speech. If a lax supervisor lets them go two hours without reminding them to badger people into spending "just a few dollars more", they feel like they've been on an exotic holiday.

Most of the people who work in the video store are very much like this. They are helpful and attentive, and they hate to bust up the rapport they've built with you by trying to sell you a premium program you don't want. They offer it, when they feel the eyes of Big Brother on their back. You politely refuse. They drop the awkward subject, give you your movie, and bid you a pleasant good night.

Not so with the girl we hate. This TV child genius wannabe seems to take a twisted sort of pride in how many times, and how many ways, she can make you say no. She sets her add-on-sales teeth into you like a pit bull terrier. It's not only that she won't take no for an answer and goes right on pitching at you; it's the way she talks at you like she is a fountain of simple wisdom. She stares at you all the while with a look on her face that expects you to see the light at any moment and realize that she really is the wise one in the transaction, whose sound reasoning cannot be denied by any amount of mature reflection.

I may not be a genius myself, or play one on TV, or wish I played one on TV, but I do generally know what I want, and what I don't want. When I go into the video store it is generally because I want to rent a movie and get home in time to watch it before bed. I'm pretty sure I don't want to spend the evening arguing with a very average twenty-year-old, who's pretending to be a very above average twelve-year-old, about how many bonus points I am likely to accrue through the normal course of keeping myself entertained. Neither do I want to be painted as a fool who will be wasting all of those precious points if I don't sign up right now for the rewards program and pay the $10 annual fee. Gwen doesn't like it when I'm painted as a fool either (unless, of course, she is the painter).

Gwen won't even respond to the video girl's sales pitch. If anything, she is the majority owner of our hatred for that particular clerk. Last time we went to rent a movie, Gwen got in line behind a customer who was filling out a new membership form rather than going to the hated girl, who had no customers in front of her register. When the girl saw us, she waved to attract Gwen's

43

attention and shouted out, "I can help you over here."

Gwen looked her straight in the eye and told her calmly, "No, you can't."

I guess the girl thought Gwen didn't understand her, because she said, "Ma'am, I can ring you up at this register."

Gwen made really strong eye contact with her again. "No. You're not allowed to ring me up," she said. Then she turned back and looked straight ahead at the guy copying down his license number in front of her.

The girl stood there for a minute, trying to make sense of it all. After that, she went away to stare at the new release wall or something. I was pretending to look at the huge box of Junior Mints all the while, but I saw the whole thing. It was great.

Gwen didn't have to hear any sales pitch that night. Unlike me, and unlike the video store girl, I think Gwen might actually be a genius.

6.
Too Productive to be Professional

You may have gotten the idea by now that my job is not very rewarding. That is true. In fact, with each passing day it gets more difficult to want to show up in the morning. It was getting to the point where it was tempting to call in sick every so often, just for a break from the strain of motivating myself to go in. The problem is that I don't get paid for sick time. So, I had to come up with a new strategy.

This is what I do to get through the work week. It's so simple that I'm kind of ashamed that I didn't think of it sooner. When I get to the accounting office, I pretend that I'm actually a prisoner in the state correctional system. Up till I lucked out and got this work release job, I was stuck in the joint 24-7. I had serial murderers coming at me with shivs, and big, bad dudes wanting me to pay them for protection with cigarettes and other commodities that a con like myself would rather not list. Through the grace of God, and my exemplary good conduct in hiking up my skirt and fleeing from every potential prison-yard conflict, I was granted the wonderful reprieve of work release.

It's certainly a better environment in the accounting office than it was in the "big house." While I still have to look over my shoulder at all times, at least I'm not looking out for a sock full of ball bearings arching down toward my skull. Best of all, I'm not the acknowledged property of a snaggletoothed beefcake with a tattoo on his forehead. Thanks to the warden's eye for talent, I'm not Bruiser's bitch; I'm the Education Industrial Complex's bitch, which, in the short run, is a far less traumatic thing to be.

There are two main reasons why the Education Industrial Complex has put me in with the group of employees that are its bitches. The first is obvious: I'm a temp. A temp is every permanent employee's bitch. When the regular workers are done with a temp, maybe the institution can find a minute to slap him around, if he's not too used up already to be worth the time. The other reason I am what I am is slightly less obvious: I don't have an advanced degree.

The Education Industrial Complex isn't quite as abrupt at manhandling you as I imagine Bruiser would be. It just kind of massages you toward where it wants you to be. If I were to stay employed within the Educational Industrial Complex for the long run, it would likely massage me right into that graduate degree before I had a clue about what was happening.

In spite of the fact that I would not have been given this assignment had I lacked a B.A., I could do my job, spying on Marge Meko, every bit as well without one. Had I become a father at 16, lived in a trailer, and spent the next 10 years changing diapers (of multiple children), I have no doubt that I would have been better prepared to deal with Marge Meko than I am now.

Marge Meko has no degree of any kind. Some people look down their noses at Marge Meko because of her lack of education, but they only do it behind her back. No one's brave enough to look down into her face. She has no responsibilities, she's accountable to no one, she makes as much, or more, than many of the people who look down at her from behind, and she leaves her work behind when she goes home—if indeed she had anything to leave in the first place. You tell me, who's the smart one?

Steve, on the other hand, has an MBA. He has a bachelor's in accounting and an MBA. He is also a CPA. I think this certification's greatest value to Steve is that it has increased the number of initials after his name from five to eight—an increase of

60 percent, if my non-MBA math skills do not fail me. I can't say what amount of actual accounting training Steve's vast education has lent him, because if he does any actual accounting for the school, he does it behind closed doors.

We all have seen people use their advanced education as a springboard to do wonderful things for humanity. I don't know that I can say that Steve's education has been such a boon to civilization. What I do know about Steve's education is that none of it taught him how to be in charge of other people. All those years of schooling took Steve's woefully underdeveloped leadership skills, dug a hole for them, buried them, pretended that they were never important in the first place, and promised never to speak of them again. And those years kept their word, kept it to the point that if it ever occurred to Steve that he needed to recover those skills, stunted as they were, he would not have the slightest idea where to start digging.

Neither Steve nor Marge Meko is the kind of person you would want to have to perform brain surgery on you. Steve has a ton more formal education; Marge is a remarkable, self-taught manipulator. Between them, they have just enough competence to hide their collective cornucopia of errors from a pack of ostriches who aren't looking for them and would trip over them a dozen times before they could be bothered to notice them. So I guess they're both about as smart as they have to be.

Not that it matters, but if the Armageddon comes in our lifetimes, I would rather be in Marge Meko's tribe of post-apocalyptic mutants than in any other. Marge is a proven survivor. When it's all said and done, she will be battling with the cockroaches for supremacy of the earth. We have a few people around here who look like they're the type who hoard supplies in their basements, preparing for the cataclysm. Poor saps, Marge Meko knows who they are and where they live. When that happy day comes, and they are sitting pretty in their mole holes, Marge and her gang (if she allows any hangers-on) will come sniff them out, dig them up, and be living high on their canned goods before they even know what hit them. They'll have to talk nice and pretty to her if they hope to get a bite of their own provisions.

What does it mean when your job leaves you fantasizing about the apocalypse? That's a rhetorical question, by the way.

One of the smartest people I've met at Appalachian Downslope College is a young lady named Renee. She works in the registrar's office. One day I got volunteered to go over there and help her stuff envelopes. They were sending out some special announcement to all the students and they advertised for help among the various offices. I guess the fact that I was the only person sent to help was Steve's way of letting me know that I rated well as envelope fodder. It was fine by me, though. The day away from Steve and Marge Meko ranked up there as one of my top three Christmases.

It doesn't take a lot of concentration to stuff envelopes, so Renee and I had plenty of chance to converse. She's six years younger than me, and a permanent employee, but that's not anything to be jealous about. She's called an office manager; I soon figured out that she singlehandedly keeps the registrar's office afloat.

The day I was there, nearly everybody else was in a great big, long meeting. They were all in a conference room, behind a closed door—all the registrars, vice registrars, assistant registrars, and various other offshoots of that important word that the office requires. Meanwhile, Renee was left alone to execute the crucial mailing, which was just the way she wanted it. She was happy to have them all out of her hair, because she was indulging in a secret rite: efficiency.

Being the groundbreaking institution that it is, Appalachian Downslope College was doing what it had done for years: patterning its operations after those of a large eastern university.

48

This doesn't always serve Downslope well, because the tools of the big institution don't always fit the little guy so well. In this case, the database that the large eastern university used to catalogue its students' names and addresses was bulky, inflexible, and absolutely not open to the slightest customization. In short, it was completely unsuited to the needs of a smaller institution. As a result, its use led to numerous errors in tracking down students, and piles and piles of returned mail. Yet it was favored by the large university; therefore it must be state of the art; therefore Appalachian Downslope College had strained every fiber of its budget to purchase it, and has ever since worn it as a chip on its increasingly hunched shoulder.

As it was Renee's job to co-ordinate the mass mailings of the registrar, she was in a fine position to see how poorly the system worked at providing useful information to the more intimate organization. As it was not Renee's job to point out flaws in any very expensive, sacred cows, she was not in a fine position to complain about it. As it was also her job to deal with the angry students who never received important notices, she was given ample motivation to circumvent the system in order to execute, with any hope of success, the part of her job first mentioned.

While her many bosses cloistered themselves in a meeting room for strategic planning and other pleasant chit-chat, Renee set about building a shadow system that would make her job possible to do, and incidentally, insulate all the generals, huddled over their secret battle plans and dessert recipes, from rumblings of discontent among their constituents. While the intelligencia schemed, in ignorant bliss, Renee built her own database. Renee's database was not shiny or expensive, but it was clever, and it fit the situation. It did the unthinkable: it allowed Renee to keep accurate records.

Renee's homemade database could not do one very important thing. It could not pretend to be the big, clumsy database that the college had sold its soul to get. Hence, Renee took up a position that was at the opposite pole to Marge Meko. While Marge Meko casually did things that she knew were wrong, or at least stood an equal chance of being wrong as they did of being right, and never once found it necessary to look behind her, Renee ran an obstacle course in order to do things right, and couldn't stop looking over her shoulder for a pointed finger of accusation.

"So," I said to Renee as I laid another filled envelope on the pile, "you basically have to do all your effective work when nobody is looking. Doesn't that get annoying?"

"It's not so bad," she said. "They have a lot of meetings. That gives me enough time to run my queries and get the lists I need. The good thing is that my system is much more time efficient than the school's is, so I can get everything done quickly, and still have plenty of time left to pretend I'm using the official system. I make sure I'm always printing out reports from the official system whenever anybody comes by."

"Would those reports be necessary to do the mailing, even if you were using the school's database for it?"

"Oh no," she said. "The reports just make people feel like they're getting their money's worth. See that filing cabinet over there?" She pointed to five foot vertical file. "I run a good handful of reports every week and keep them stocked up in that bad boy. That way, whenever anybody gets to feeling insecure, they can go over and reassure themselves that we are on the cutting edge of record-keeping technology."

"That whole thing's full of useless reports?" I asked.

She smiled. "Jam packed."

"And the people who take comfort in them don't try to use them?"

"They're not for using. They're for looking at, like a really old coin collection. One time the registrar even showed them off to the provost. Word has it she got a raise shortly after. And who can argue with that? They're a pretty impressive bunch a reports."

"They must be."

"You just reminded me," she said, "I've got to remember to weed that cabinet out and make a little more room. It's getting a little tight and they're threatening to buy me another one."

"Two full cabinets might just get somebody around here a promotion," I said. She knew I wasn't talking about her, but she smiled anyway.

"Do you ever join in their meetings?" I asked.

"I've never been invited."

"Why not?"

"The meetings are for professional staff."

"You're not professional staff?"

"No," she said. "I suppose I'm not. It's not like anybody comes around and points to people and says, 'You're professional staff. You're not professional staff.' It's an unspoken thing, but whenever the registrar wants to tout her professional staff, you can tell who she's referring to, and I'm not on that list."

"How can that be?" I asked. "You're title has the word *manager* right in it. Have you got a degree?"

"Only a B.S., in business."

"Only?"

She rolled her eyes as if I hadn't been paying attention. "Take a good look around you. These folks are all about buying what their selling."

"There's no doubt about that. But tell me, in what other line of work would a college grad with *manager* in their title not be considered a professional?"

She shrugged. "I don't know. Maybe this is the only one. I'm only 23. I don't have a lot of experience out in the real world."

"That puts you on par with most of the professional staff huddled in the next room."

She shrugged. "Hey, they're doing all right for themselves.

Everybody's real world is the one in which they are a success."

"Why don't you leave, find the real world where you can at least be considered professional?"

"Why don't you?" she asked.

It was a fair question. "I'm on vacation from the real world," I told her. "I'll go back after a while, but for now this is kind of a relaxing break, even if stuffing envelopes is the most challenging and creative task I've done in three weeks. When I graduated I went right into retail management. I was in that for six years, until it finally beat the hell out me. When I recover from the bruises, and maybe find a less bumpy road, I'll go back to the real world. Besides, they'll kick me out of here before too long."

"Why is that?'

"Because I've never been a very good student, I don't like being a babysitter, and I won't stand for being made into a eunuch."

"So that's what they do in the biology lab." She nodded with newfound understanding. "Back in my day we just dissected frogs."

"Yeah," I said. "A lot can change in a week."

"Shows how much you know." She avoided the temptation to stick out her tongue at me. "It was a good two years if it was a day."

Now, I don't want you to get the idea that Renee and I were flirting. That would be the wrong idea. We were just trading some lighthearted banter. Sure, Renee has her attractive qualities, but I am completely devoted to Gwen. If, hypothetically, there were no Gwen in the picture, I might have been flirting with Renee. But as things are, I was not. I just wanted to make sure that was understood.

"You haven't answered the question yet," I reminded her. "Why do you stay here?"

"Sometimes I think I should leave," she replied. "But I

don't think I could handle the guilt."

"What?" I looked at her like she were crazy. I'm pretty good with that look. I should be; I get it enough from Gwen.

"I feel like I'd be leaving them in the lurch." She nodded toward the meeting room as she spoke.

"It'd do them good to have a little of the heavy lifting to do for a change."

"I'm not sure they'd know where to begin," she said with real concern for them.

"They'd have to learn. They're highly educated people after all."

"That's what I'm afraid of," she said. "I've been noticing since I started working here that some highly educated people don't really like learning how to *do* things. They prefer lofty concepts, learning how to follow trends, and figuring out what the conventional wisdom is."

"The stuff of long meetings," I interrupted.

"I only just realized when I started this job that I didn't know how to *do* anything. But since I was the least educated, it fell upon me to figure out *how* to do things. Around here, someone with my education is pretty easy to replace. Getting things done was the only tool I had to hang on with. Fortunately, I don't mind figuring things out on my own."

"I'm not saying they won't have a tough time when you're gone, but why do you care so much about that? It's not your problem. You'll be gone."

"I care so much about it because I like them," she said. "Yeah, maybe they don't like to get their hands dirty too much, but they're basically good people. They've always been nice to me."

"But they treat you like you're second class."

"Maybe they do. But I have a hard time believing this is the only line of work where that kind of thing happens. The people at the top of the totem pole always think highly of themselves.

53

Besides, it's their world; they can do what they want. I didn't have to come here, and I don't have to stay here. I took this job of my own free will; nobody held a gun to my head. If I didn't understand it then, I very quickly learned exactly what is valued here. I don't have it; they do. I can't just expect them to rearrange the way their whole world works because I decided to try and live in it."

"They could change it a little. They don't even seem to have a clue about how much you do."

"They can't afford to worry about that. Look, their business is higher education. It's good to believe in your business. They focus on what they have to focus on, and they hire someone like me to take care of the rest. They use a system that serves their cause. It's only natural, and I can't bring myself to hold it against them."

She was making some good points, but I wasn't letting her know that. "You can't work here forever," I said.

"Neither can you," she replied. "Are there a lot of job openings for eunuchs these days?"

"Mostly just temporary assignments," I said.

Renee and I had to pace ourselves to make the envelope stuffing last out the afternoon. Actually, I had to beg her to slow down. She's so conscientious that she would have finished up and gotten a whole pile of other work done. I'd had such an unusually pleasant day helping her that I couldn't bear to be sent back into the dreary realm of Marge Meko and Steve.

Renee agreed to stretch the job out, for which I am very grateful. It was my best day so far at Appalachian Downslope College, and not because Renee is cute. I didn't notice that nearly as much as I might have if I were single. It was a good day because Renee is level-headed, and that was such a welcome relief. She showed me a new perspective and gave me something to think about. Maybe the true believers really are very good people. I'm sure good people get mixed up in cults sometimes. It's something to consider.

At the end of the day Renee printed some random reports off the big, unwieldy database. She arranged the pages as if it were a bundle of great importance. I opened the filing cabinet for her and she found them a cozy place, where their newness would be conspicuous. All the nice people would be able to sleep easy. All was well with the world.

7.

High Art v. Pornography, Verdict: Love

Whenever I meet a woman like Renee—smart, witty, attractive—I end up comparing her to Gwen. I don't know if this makes me a good boyfriend or a bad one. I'm not emotionally equipped to figure that out. It's just what I do. Often, I end up thinking back to when I first met Gwen. It's kind of fun harkening back to those exciting days, except that it means I have to remember what it was like working retail management, and that can be a buzz kill.

Before my stint in retail management I was not quite so jumpy as I am now. In retail management, you develop a habit of looking over your shoulder, and ducking into a crouch at odd times, as though you might be expecting somebody to suddenly lunge at you. There's good reason for it though; there are always a fair amount of brickbats flying through the airspace of retail management.

For most of that time I worked for a large retail book chain. I don't like to say the name because it raises the risk of post traumatic syndrome. All I can say is: some bad shit went down. But every cloud has its silver lining, and if the cloud doesn't actually choke you to death, you might live to enjoy the silver lining. My silver lining from those overcast days is Gwen. I thought she was cute the day I hired her. I'm not saying that influenced my decision to hire her, but it didn't influence me not to hire her either.

Most of the employees were college-aged, and I wasn't

much older myself. If you think a young man in his twenties can hold himself aloof from the college women who work for him, well, you were never that guy, were you? Actually, most of the young women, and for that matter, the young men, who worked for me thought I was a bastard for the first six weeks. They felt I rode them too hard and expected too much of them too soon. Some of them even thought that I was belittling their efforts to climb the learning curve of bookselling.

I wasn't. I merely wanted them to become good at what they did, so that they could be comfortable with it, and self-sufficient. In the vast majority of cases, it worked. After those six weeks, I wasn't such a bastard anymore. By then they had become comfortable enough to realize that my satire was not aimed at them, but at the circumstances of retail life, which we would have to endure together.

After another six weeks, I began to actually be kind of cool. The same things I'd said and done 12 weeks ago weren't mean and hurtful anymore. They were a little bit funny. They were things with which a comfortable retail worker could identify. After three months of steady rowing, we were finally in the same boat. Between the sea of customers and the storming of the corporate offices, we needed to be able to pull together; to do that, we had to be able to laugh together at the world in which we toiled.

Every once in a while, one of the female employees, who had gotten past the period in which I was nothing but an authoritarian jerk, would come to the wholly reasonable conclusion that I was even more than kind of cool. Before you get the idea that I was nothing more than a predator, who used his position to take advantage of innocent young girls, I will tell you that it didn't happen that often. Most of the times it did happen, I discouraged any non-professional notions the young lady might be developing about me. Still, every man has his failings, and there were a couple of times when my weakness for the combination of a sly smile and a witty remark got the best of me.

I won't go into detail because this is not a kiss-and-tell exposé, and besides that, it would have needed a lot more kissing to make it worth telling. No one was taken advantage of, unless it was me. All that ended, ended well enough so that no one was scarred and everybody went on happily with their lives. Then Gwen came along.

Gwen had me turned so inside out from the very first that I couldn't even make her believe I was a cruel martinet past the first week. Gwen had to learn to become a good bookseller pretty much on her own, as I was generally tongue-tied in her presence. Also, the back of my neck was often abnormally warm.

It took me those first six weeks to prove to Gwen that I wasn't a bumbler, waiting to be ferreted out of the system by a series of poor sales reports. I was actually pretty fair at what I did, and by the time I finally got the last knot out of my stomach, I was able to begin to look like it too. Then, I found that I could begin to speak to her intelligibly. Eventually, I discovered that I had reached the level where I could actually flirt with her. That, I think, was my happiest day in retail.

It was also, though I didn't realize it at the time, the beginning of the end of my retail career. On the day that I was sure that what I was doing with Gwen was real flirting, I had accomplished the greatest feat of my retail life. I had accomplished every wonderful thing that I was ever going to accomplish in retail. I hadn't had any lofty goals when I first fell into the retail management track. Seriously, how do you formulate lofty goals when you're falling? It's hard to get to be the life of any kind of party by bragging about how many portable book lights you moved last quarter. I guess, all along, my loftiest goal had been to find a way out of retail management, and I wasn't too near attaining that one yet.

So flirting with Gwen was a big milestone for me. I

figured if I could really get her to like me, I might turn out to be the biggest retail management success story of all time. Or, I could forget all about her, and really buckle down for the next 10 or 15 years and try to make district manager, at which point I would have the inestimable pleasure of spending my time keeping track of how many portable book lights everybody in the state had moved last quarter. Well, most of those portable book lights turn out to be junk anyway.

Soon, I was flirting on a regular basis with Gwen, but that, in itself, was no guarantee of a happy ending to the story. Gwen's a good flirt. She can keep the best of men enthralled with her banter. I've seen women look at her with cow eyes when she really gets going. There's just something magnetic about her presence. That's not the kind of charm that's easy to hide under a bushel.

What I'm trying to say is that I was not the only kid in whose eyes Gwen had planted stars. She flirted with all her co-workers, most of the customers, and a simple majority of the people we suspected of shoplifting. Those who felt strong enough to hold their own, flirted back. The rest either turned to jelly and melted or silently handed over the magazine they had hidden in their pants and walked away defeated. The fact that I had stopped turning to jelly was good progress, but it did not give any assurance that I had surged ahead of the more hardened petty larcenists in Gwen's popular heart.

It was difficult to know where Gwen's heart really was. Every man thought they had it firmly in hand for the duration of his face time with her. Inevitably, she would go away to shower her smile upon someone else, and every man would find his feeble hands empty. She didn't even have to smile at somebody else; she could smile at an inanimate object, anything that wasn't you, and you'd feel the pain of losing her. One time she smiled at a poster of Mark Twain, promoting Banned Books Week. Have you ever harbored a red hot jealousy against Mark Twain? And not because

59

of his great gifts, or his wealth, or his fame, but because your heartthrob smiled at his likeness? Well, my friend, I have, and it took a good deal of self restraint not to put my fist through that smug, paper face of his. Yes, it's ridiculous, and after a few days had cooled me down I went by and apologized to him. But our relationship has never been quite the same.

In the race for Gwen's affections, the artist's rendition of Mark Twain and I were stuck with the pack. As hard as I tried, I could not make up any ground. Then, one night, a very zealous young man stepped briefly into our lives and gave me the boost I needed. It was the last thing he had intended upon doing that evening.

Allow me to give you a little helpful background. As a big, chain store, we carried a good selection of bulky, pricey, art books. They covered a wide range of artistic media and wide range of artists. Some of the artists were famous and some were not. Some were painters, some were sculptors, some photographers, what have you. The guy who started all the trouble was black and white photographer of very little fame, named Jack Callum.

Jack Callum, among his other artistic pursuits, had a penchant for taking photographs of people in the nude. As far as nudes went, it seems that old Jack was not content with stripping down a woman, throwing her on a sofa and snapping a few pics. Jack liked his nudes to be doing something. In fact, it seems as if Jack were never happier than when he could get a good, candid shot of a naked person doing something that you or I might do on any given day, with our clothes on. For example, I think Jack would have been pleased as punch to get an action shot of any random person loading the dishwasher in the nude. I can't say that I get what Jack was trying to say with his nudes, but then I have never burdened myself with the expectation that I would get the point of art.

Well, if Jack had just limited himself to natural art of

homemakers doing their chores I don't suppose there'd have been much trouble. But Jack went ahead and dived into sociology as a companion for his art. Jack decided that he was the man to make his name documenting the daily activities of naked families. For his masterwork on the subject, he chose a nice, big family, with plenty of children. This is where old Jack's art started to make some collars get awfully tight.

I don't remember the title of the book, and I'm not sure I even knew it existed, let alone that we had it on our shelves, before the evening in question. Suddenly, this collection of photographs of parents and children engaged in the most routine of domestic activities became the most important book in the store. I don't know what it is about being nude when hanging the laundry out on the clothes line that magically transforms the act from household drudgery into high art, but there must be something to it, because, for a while at least, just such a tableau as that was causing quite a sensation.

It seems as though there is, in the minds of some, a very tiny space between high art and pornography. Now, I don't know enough about high art or pornography to have credibly accused the photographs in this book of having been either, but the experts on both sides were busy passing their assessments, and those assessments were trickling right down upon my head. The high art people were being quiet, as they were free to take this book home with them and do whatever one does with pictures of naked families playing board games.

The pornography experts, which in a coincidence I won't ever understand, turned out to be the ones who never willingly looked at pornography in all their lives, were less content. The pornography people had two things that should never be taken together in a functional society: they had a grudge, and they had a leader. Forgive me, but I also forget the leader's name. What's more important, I think, than his name, was the fact that he had the keys to a radio station. I don't know how, or where, this man got on the air, but he did, and believe it or not, some of God's sheep listened to him. How he discovered old Jack's book of naked photos, I can't imagine. And how he determined that Jack's pictures were pornographic, I don't dare to guess, as I'm sure he did not willingly look at them. Be that as it may, he condemned Jack's book as pornography, and worse yet, *child* pornography.

That would have been one thing, and I'd happily have left him to his opinion. I'd have just as happily left old Jack and his friends to their opinions, and even the nude family to theirs, although I think one has to question the collective mental capacity of a family who goes out to pick wild raspberries without any clothes on. But the leader of the pornography faction was not content merely to call a spade a spade, as he saw it. He demanded action; he wanted that evil book burned, and anyone who'd had anything to do with it flogged, or vice versa. Since nobody else was likely to do anything he wanted them to do, he demanded action of his small flock of listeners.

This is how Gwen and I first met one of the pornography sect leader's loyal radio listeners, and how the whole thing blossomed into love. It was about an hour before closing on a week night in the middle of summer. Very few customers, and fewer employees, remained in the store. Gwen, and another part-time employee named James were at the front, manning the nearly silent cash registers. I had just visited the front of the store to deliver a roll of quarters or some such routine task, and was headed back to the office to get a head start on the day's reconciliation when James called me over to his register.

There was a man, probably a few years younger than myself, on the opposite side of the counter from James. James indicated that this customer wished to speak to whomever was in charge. This was not too alarming; customers want to speak to whomever is in charge every day, and mostly their motives for doing so are quite benign. Sometimes they have something bothering them that they'd like to complain about, but sometimes they just want to complement the service a particular bookseller gave them. Usually, when they have a bone to pick with you, they don't try very hard to hide it. They let it out to the first employee they find, and that employee telegraphs it to you. James wasn't sending me any trouble warnings, so I had no reason to believe that any unpleasant feelings had been raised.

I went over and asked the young man what I could help him with. I suppose I most expected him to ask if we were hiring. Little did I realize that this particular book store was the last place before hell where he wanted to work.

"I want you to call the police and tell them you're having a problem with a disruptive customer," he said.

My first thought was that he was making a complaint against someone he had run across elsewhere in the store. From time to time we had problems with kids doing nasty things in the restrooms. I prepared myself to go chase some teenagers out of the store.

"Where is he?" I asked.

"Who?"

"The disruptive customer."

"What do you mean?"

I didn't know how to make it any plainer, so I did what a retail manager does best and repeated myself. "Where is the disruptive customer?"

"Right here."

"In the store, I know. But what part of the store?"

"This part. Me. I want you to report me to the police."

"Why?"

"Because I'm being disruptive."

Confused was a better word for him. It was becoming a fine word for me as well. Disruptive, I was still not sold on, not nearly enough to get the police involved anyway.

"This level of disruptive really doesn't meet the threshold of calling the police," I told him.

This was clearly disappointing to him. "How about this?" he said. "I'm not leaving this counter until you call the police."

For a second I lost my patience. I suppose the weirdness of the situation flummoxed me a bit. "All right." I started to walk toward the nearest phone, but I regained my composure before I had taken my third step. I stopped. "If you want me to call the police, you'd better tell me what this is all about," I demanded as I turned back toward him.

"I want the police to see what kind of obscene books you're selling." That's when I saw that he had brought Jack Callum's book from the shelf and had it on the counter beside him. "It's illegal to sell obscene material in this state."

Now that I had a better idea of what he was all about, I thought I could begin to deal with him. "I'm not going to call the police down here to look through some photography book."

"Well I'm not leaving until you call the police, or you remove this book from your shelves."

"Well, I'm not calling the police," I countered. "And as for taking this book off the shelf, even if I decided it was a horrible book and took it down, it'd be back up tomorrow. See, you're complaining to the wrong people. This is just one store in a huge chain. Nobody in this store gets to decide which books we want and which we don't. That gets decided at headquarters. Those are the people you have your quarrel with. There are a lot of good people in this store, just trying to make an honest living on modest wages. What you're doing now just makes their jobs harder, and it will get you nowhere." I offered him contact information for our home office.

He wanted none of it. "Are you going to call the police or not?" he asked.

"No. You're just not disrupting things that much for me to call the cops."

He was growing irritable. "What if I walked out with the book without paying?"

"Well, then I might call the police, and they'd arrest you for shoplifting. It'd probably get into all the papers, and everybody would know that you wanted that book so badly that you couldn't wait till you'd saved up enough to buy it."

This scenario did not sit well with the young zealot. He opened the book and put his hand around the edge of a stack of pages. "What if started ripping pages out?"

"Well, when the police came, they'd probably just make you buy it, which would put you in our records as having bought *that* book." Of course, this was all utter nonsense. Nobody would make him buy any book. Besides that, we didn't have any records of who bought what. In fact, if he paid cash there would be no way that anyone could link him to any particular purchase. Still, I was getting a feeling that he would buy just about any load of bull that was fed him, provided it was fed with a certain air of authority.

His hand slid out of the book and he closed the cover. "Why won't you just call the police?" he asked in exasperation.

"Just walk out that door with the book. I'll call them right away." I admit that I was starting to have fun, which was not what I should have been doing, but I hadn't asked him to thrust himself into my peaceful little world either.

Meanwhile a woman brought some magazines up to Gwen's register. The young man, weary of my intractability, turned his efforts upon her. He opened the book up to what he thought a good representative sample of its obscenity and held it up before the lady. "Have you seen the pornography they sell in this store?" he asked her.

At first, she did not understand that he was addressing her, and when she figured it out, she was a little taken aback. After all, what would you think if a complete stranger accosted you with a two-page of spread of a naked family enjoying naked family time? She got that look on her face that people get when instinct tells them to lean backward.

"That's right," he told her. "This is just the kind of trash they sell here. It's right back in the art section."

"Well, it's disgusting. They shouldn't sell books like that." She gave us all a look of shame and disappointment before dismissing us all from her thoughts and turning back to complete her purchase.

He backed off and closed the book once he had elicited such a favorable response. "No, they shouldn't, and they won't, once the cops get a good look at what's in here." He made another foray into her line of sight, this one less graphic. "Will you call the police for me, while I stay here with the book?"

Disgusted or not, this lady was not about to get her name involved in the affair that would result when the cops came to look at the naked pictures. She had her wallet out, and looked like she was planning on putting her change neatly inside, but now she took her change and tossed it, along with the wallet, randomly into her purse. "What? No, I'm sorry. I can't. I'm in an awful hurry." She hadn't appeared to be much of an athlete, but she went out the front door at what was at least a brisk jog.

Thwarted again, the young man, in his desperation, was struck with an inspiration of simple brilliance. "Can I use your phone," he asked me.

The request was such a stroke of pure genius that I was tempted to accede to it. Yet, being no more eager to have him call the police on me than I was to call the police on him, the temptation burned itself out at once. "I'm sorry," I said. "Our phones are only to be used for official store business. There's a pay phone out front."

"Then I'll have to leave the book here," he protested.

"If you've given up on the shoplifting idea," I agreed.

"And by the time the police show up, I'm sure it will have magically disappeared."

This was a new twist to me. I honestly had never thought of trying to hide the book from anyone. It was a ridiculous idea. Hiding your books is one hell of way for a bookstore to do business. Furthermore, it was just plain stupid. For better or worse, we carried this book. If anybody cared enough to investigate that question, it would be pretty easy to figure that out, no matter how deep a well I threw that particular copy down. We had stores in every city with that book on the shelf, and the publisher had plenty of records of our corporate buyers taking it. I, and the company, would come off looking pretty silly if I tried to deny that we stocked the book.

I was a little irked that he would imply that I was dim-witted enough to try such a ploy. I picked up a pen and a piece of scrap paper from the counter. "Here's what I'm going to do," I told him rather aggressively. "Not only is this book not going to disappear, if you give me your name, I'll hold it for you. That will give you three days to get the cops in here. Meanwhile, nobody but you can have this book. Now, what's your name?"

He was a bit dumbfounded by my suggestion, but apparently I had made it with enough authority that he didn't doubt my word. He told me his name was Wright, Christian Wright. I didn't raise an eyebrow. I didn't care that the name was fake, or even that it was a bad pun. All that mattered is that he remembered what it was when he came back. I rubber-banded the paper with his name to the book and put it with the other books on hold. For once, he seemed satisfied with my actions and left to make his phone call.

The incident itself was pretty much anticlimax after that. He came back with a couple of cops about 20 minutes later. He asked for his book from the hold shelf. I pretended that I had forgotten his name so that he would have to repeat it in front of the cops. I wanted to give them an idea of the world perspective with which they were dealing.

The cops didn't enjoy having the photographs stuck in their faces any more than anybody else did. Once they got an idea of what it was all about, they made Mr. Wright shut the book and put it down. The cops weren't excited about trying to mediate this dispute. While one of them took down Mr. Wright's complaint, the other went back to the reference section to see if we had a test prep guide that he'd been looking to buy.

After they were done with Mr. Wright, the cops told me that they were obliged to take the book in question as evidence for the county prosecutor. He was the one who had the plumb job of determining if we had broken any obscenity laws. I could tell the cops weren't any more envious of the county prosecutor than I was. The only one who seemed like he would have enjoyed the job was Christian Wright.

We didn't have the study guide the one cop wanted, so they left pretty quick. Christian Wright left right after them. He seemed very proud of himself. I hope he enjoyed his pride, because it turned out that he was headed for a fall. The rest of us got ready to close up shop. It had been a long night.

As we were walking to our cars after locking up, Gwen and I found ourselves going to the same corner of the parking lot. "Wow, that was a crazy night," she said to me.

"Yeah, I wonder if they'll take us all to jail tomorrow."

"That guy was serious about obscenity, wasn't he? But I thought you handled him well."

"Yeah?" A guy doesn't ignore a compliment from the likes of Gwen, even if he has nothing more gracious than "Yeah?" at hand with which to accept it.

"Yeah. I really loved it when you offered to put the book on hold for him. Did you see his face. His eyes just about popped out of his head. He was so not expecting that level of service from somebody he was about to call the cops on. It was brilliant."

"Brilliant? You think so?"

"Okay. I don't know if it was brilliant, but it was pretty cool."

Gwen had just called something I had done pretty cool, which I naturally inferred to mean that she thought I was pretty cool. This was a breakthrough accomplishment. Accordingly, I grinned from ear to ear. "Thanks."

"Listen," she said. "I know it's late, and we've all had a long day, but you did pretty good tonight and you probably deserve to have a beer bought for you."

I'm sure my grin grew, even though it was probably at record wideness already. "Probably?" was all I could think to say.

"Yeah, probably. How about Ben Franklin's?" Ben Franklin's was a pub down the street.

"Sounds great."

"Good. I'll follow you there." She got into her car and I got into mine. I doubt that she sang at the top of her lungs all the way to Ben Franklin's, but I sure as hell did.

That night at Ben Franklin's I got my first chance at some quiet, one-on-one time with Gwen. In spite of my overwhelming giddiness, I must have made the most of it. Gwen and I started hanging out together outside of work, and before I knew how I had pulled it off, we were dating. We didn't openly call it dating for some time, because I was, technically, her boss. We were just hanging out together, and whatnot.

That's the story of how Gwen and I first got together. You might want to know the whole obscenity thing turned out, so I won't leave you hanging. The next day, we got word that people just like Christian Wright had pulled similar stunts in our stores all over the country. The home office formulated some guidelines for dealing with such incidents. The guidelines could be broken down to: 1. Don't call the police just because somebody tells you to; call them if you need them. 2. Don't try to hide the book from anybody. 3. If the police do show up, co-operate with them. It all seemed pretty elementary to me.

A couple of days later, somebody who knew how to find the pornography guru's radio show informed us that they had been listening when Christian Wright called in to brag about his exploits in our store. Unfortunately for Christian, as he was recounting his story, his radio leader found fault with it. Apparently, Christian should have torn the book to shreds and been willing to incur a police record for the cause. His fearless leader, safe in his radio studio, ripped him a new you-know-what on air for being too timid. So much for Mr. Wright's smug pride.

We heard that some of the prosecutors down south got a little more involved in the fracas, but we never heard a peep from ours. A few weeks later, the book was unceremoniously returned to us and put back on the shelf. We waited to see if any of the southern authorities would take the issue to court, but we never heard of it.

We saw Christian Wright a couple more times. He came in one day and started shouting as loud as he could about how we sold pornography. Apparently, he was bruised by the verbal hiding he'd taken on the radio and wanted to show that he really did have a pair. Somebody asked him to leave, and after a few more shouted statements, he did. The customers were more confused than anything, and I think it was their blank stares that really convinced Christian to go.

He came by one other time that I know of, but I don't really remember what he did that time. He may have come in just to buy something, for all I know. After that, he disappeared. I think we eventually returned the book to the publisher because its sales were so poor. Like Christian Wright, Jack Callum and his naked families just sort of faded away.

The bunch of them are all but forgotten now. I say "all but" because I haven't forgotten them. I remember Christian and Jack fondly. You might think that none of them made any great difference in the world. I disagree. They made a huge difference; they got me Gwen.

8.
Gramps Tears off a Piece

Things at work have taken an ugly turn. That would be bad enough if I could blame this fresh ugliness on Marge Meko and Steve, but I can't. The Boris and Natasha of my workday didn't star in this episode, so I had to stumble into trouble without their help.

It all has to do with my friend Renee, the one I helped to stuff envelopes. I'll put it right out in the open, from the top. True: I think she's cute as button. True: She's loads of fun to talk to, and a fellow can find himself flirting a little bit with her before he knows what he's doing. Also true: my heart belongs to Gwen, absolutely and completely. Gwen is everything a man could ever want in a woman. I wouldn't trade her for a super model with a Ph.D. and box seats at the Super Bowl. But, if Gwen weren't in the picture, if I'd never found her, I'd definitely be interested in Renee. But that's neither here nor there, because I did find Gwen, and that's the end of it.

I guess I'll just tell you what happened. It all started when I found out about the annual staff picnic. Apparently, on one summer Friday, all the college employees, who care to do it, meet up on the lawn behind the dining hall. Some of the food service people roll out a big barbeque grill, cook up some of the finest meats left over from the previous school year, and serve a picnic lunch to everybody. They set out plastic tables and chairs, and all kinds of such amenities to show appreciation for another year's hard work by the staff. As I understand it, it's usually run like a pot luck, in order that there be more food available than the surplus burgers, at no additional expense. This year, however, the college splurged on potato salad, which is to say that some of the students didn't eat their quota of potatoes before finals. The result of this happy circumstance was that no one was saddled with the requirement of bringing food from home for their appreciation picnic, and better still, no one was burdened with making a show of enjoying their co-workers' dubious concoctions.

Marge Meko spent the better part of a week trying to convince me that I wasn't invited to the picnic. I made the mistake of reading the flyer for the picnic in front of her. The minute she saw this, she waddled right up to me as fast as her webbed feet could manage. "Don't start thinking you're invited to that, cause you're not," she let me know.

"I didn't know you were on the picnic committee, Marge," I said. "It's not like you to volunteer for extra work."

"Very funny." She made a grotesque face (meaning, more grotesque than normal) at me. "But it doesn't change the fact that you're not invited."

"Oh, I don't know about that, Marge. It does say, '*All* college staff.'" I underlined the words with my finger.

"Ha!" Marge scoffed. "You think you're college staff? You're nothing but a lousy temp. This event is a reward for a whole year of hard work. Why would anyone want to invite Lazy Temp Gary Gray, who's only been here a few months and hasn't done a lick of work the whole time, and doesn't even know the first thing about how things work around here anyway."

"You forgot about how I try to blame my shortcomings on other people," I volunteered.

"No. I didn't forget; I just ran out of breath."

"Well, Marge, I have to thank you. You've helped me make up my mind. I'm definitely going to the picnic."

"You'd better not. They'll kick you out."

73

"They might, but that's just the chance I'm going to have to take." With that I walked confidently to my desk and sat down. I hummed a happy tune to myself and made sure to look busy. Out of the corner of my eye I could see Marge Meko stalk back to her chair. She sat down heavily and pulled out a word search puzzle book. Apparently, she was mentally distracted, because I didn't see her circle many hidden words. Every so often, she shot me a wonderfully agitated, dirty look.

In spite of my apparent confidence, Marge Meko had set me to thinking. Maybe the picnic wasn't for temps after all. It would be a little awkward if I went all the way over there, rolled up to the buffet line, and was asked to leave just as my surplus burger landed on its surplus bun. Of course, I could have asked somebody who really knew if I were welcome at the shindig, but that just seemed too difficult for some reason. Besides, what was I worried about anyway? These were college faculty and staff, not army rangers; they weren't going to put up resistance to anybody who decided to crash their party. Dirty looks were the most I had to fear, and Marge Meko was helping me to practice ignoring them all the time.

My determination to attend the picnic was not the result of my craving for freezer-burned beef. If it had been a free, public picnic, I'm sure I wouldn't have given a thought to going. I was set on going because it was a college picnic. Think about it; my pay was poor, I got no benefits, and even less respect; the least that the college owed me was an extended lunch in the summer sun. I didn't care if the burger were crappy; it was one more of the precious few things I would get out of this place. Past its expiration date or not, this college owed me that ground beef patty. That's why I was so determined to go to the picnic.

If you're thinking that the turn for the worse I mentioned earlier had something to do with me getting kicked out of the picnic after all, you're wrong. In spite of Marge Meko's strenuous efforts to discourage me from attending, I went to the picnic. Not only did no one attempt to kick me out, although I'm sure Marge Meko spent her lunch trying to raise a coalition against me, no one even bothered to cast a dirty look my way. For the most part, they had no idea I was even there. Those who did notice me, had no clue who I was, and certainly did not care to know.

I went through the food line without being noticed by anyone. Even the guy whose job it was to lower the burger onto my bun with his spatula almost missed my plate entirely, he was so disinterested in my presence before him. I was not daunted in the least until after I had gotten all of my food and turned around to survey the array of tables spread out across the patio. By the time I got my plate, the tables were nearly filled, with only an odd empty chair here and there. Aside from Steve and Marge Meko, with whom I had no desire to sit, I knew some of the people only slightly, and most of them not at all. I had almost resigned myself to the necessity of barging in on some table's collegiate clique when I noticed an arm raised high above all the heads, waving. In the next instant, I realized that the arm was waving at me, and, better still, it belonged to my friend Renee.

Renee was waving me toward an open chair at the table where she sat. This was a great boost to my spirits, partly because it meant that I did not have to insert myself into a place at a table where I was not wanted, and partly too, because, well, when a pretty girl picks you out of a crowd and waves you over to her table, it makes you feel good.

I made my way to the table and sat down next to Renee, feeling pretty good about how the picnic had treated me so far. Recall that this was before I had a chance to bite into my burger. Renee was seated with other people from her department, none of whom I knew. It didn't really matter, as Renee and I were soon deeply engaged in our own exclusive conversation. I remember thinking to myself that we were probably being rude to the others at the table, ignoring them as completely as we were, but I don't remember caring. I had such a good time talking to Renee, I hardly noticed that my burger was nearly raw, or that the potato salad had a funky aftertaste. I remember those details only in bits and pieces.

We probably could have sat there and talked for hours, had not some college bigwig felt the need to interrupt us with a speech to commemorate the picnic. He went on and on about all the hard work we had done over the past year, and how he could see the results already blossoming into fruition. I hadn't been there a year ago, but if the parts of the place I saw were that much better than they'd been a year ago, I was glad I'd missed seeing them back then.

Renee and I rolled our eyes at the steady stream of treacle. It was all too much to swallow, until he got to his last statement. He should have started with that sentence; it was the one that told us that we were all free to take the remainder of the afternoon off. One of the stalwarts from the faculty suggested that it might be a good idea to get an early start on happy hour. Since the faculty didn't have set hours like the staff did, professors were at liberty to get a head start on happy hour any time they did not have a class. It was well known to everybody, except the temp, that this particular professor was wont to make the most of his liberties.

A small, hardy group coalesced around the idea of happy hour. I didn't know any of them, which made up my mind to go home. It was a warm afternoon and the thought of getting into the apartment complex pool before the after-work crowd was agreeable to me.

"Wanna go?" Renee asked with her eyes bright and shiny.

"To happy hour?"

"Yeah. It could be fun." The word fun seemed to write itself across her eyes.

"Sure. I got nothing better to do."

Guess what: I didn't go swimming that afternoon. I went to

happy hour with Renee and a handful of faculty and staff that I didn't know. It wasn't so bad at first. The drinkers were actually the more sociable of the college people. We sat at a large, round table, and everyone talked freely with everyone else. Even when they found out that I was just a temp, I was not made an outcast. Sitting around drinking, we were just a random group of people.

The lady on my right was a history professor. She was very nice, and pretty interesting. Since she was a history professor, I didn't find it at all unusual that she was wearing clothes she must have bought 40 years ago, when she was a flower child. On the other side of Renee was the head of the math department. If you saw him out of the corner of your eye, you'd be surprised that someone so young could be the head of a college department. But once you got a good look at him you realized that he wasn't that young at all. The corners of his face showed his true age, which was clearly much greater than he wished it, by the way he used his long, wavy hair, his deep tan, and frequent visits to a Bowflex machine to mask it. He made himself seem younger too, by his easy familiarity with us, and the interest he showed in our hardscrabble lives.

Finding these people to be so friendly was a pleasant surprise, but I took every advantage of lulls in the group conversation to renew my one-on-one talks with Renee. As we sipped our drinks her eyes seemed to grow in their luster, and I felt ever warmer and more content. I should have seen red flags the moment we made fun of each other's license photos, but I was having too much fun. I wanted to go on feeling this fresh warmth, and bask in the light of those eyes.

It was only when I excused myself to go stand in front of the urinal that the permanent dose of smelling salts that is the men's room made my head vibrate on top of my neck and woke me from my little world of make believe. There's nothing like a visit to the urinal to slow things down and force a man to think;

you really can't rush a sojourn at the urinal.

For the first time in hours I was thinking, and what I was thinking was not good. Renee and I were flirting like two people who will not long be content with flirting. In a different world I could kick up my feet and go along for as far as this ride would take me, but not in this one. It had been fun, getting swept up in the moment, but there had to be an end to it, and soon. Renee was a great girl, but I wasn't about to risk Gwen for anything, not any more than I already had.

I had to get out of this. My first impulse was to make an excuse for leaving as soon as I got back to the table. This would not do though. It would only leave Renee hanging, wondering what had sent me away, and encourage her to seek answers from me later on. Instead, I had to go back out and sit down. I had to let her know about Gwen, and prove that I could talk to her without flirting, just the same as I talked to the others. I had to stop this little snowball I had started rolling down hill, and I had to do it today.

I zipped up with the resolve of a man on a mission. Normally, I like to skip over the mundane things and get on with the story, but I don't want you to get sidetracked by wondering about it, so just one unnecessary detail to get you out of the men's room: I washed my hands. Now then, if we can move along, I went back out, sat down, claimed Renee's full attention, and immediately began to suffer mission creep.

The minute I looked at Renee's face, it hit me how awkward it would be to straight out tell her that we couldn't go on flirting in this shameless manner. Flirting is always an open secret between the people doing it. You know when you're flirting; you especially know it when you're flirting like there's no tomorrow. But when the person with whom you are flirting points out that you are flirting, what is the first thing you do? You deny it. Your denial is a completely transparent sham, but you deny it all the same. You deny it because you don't want to be the vulnerable one who admits romantic feelings first. You don't want to be the fool who was flirting all by yourself.

The only way I could approach the flirting issue head on with Renee was to be the one to come out and confess that I was flirting with her. Then, she might admit that she was flirting too, and we could put the proper kibosh on things before they got messy. The problem with that plan was that it's difficult to tell the girl, with whom you've been flirting like mad, that you're going to have to stop this behavior cold turkey, because although it somehow did not come up in your detailed conversation, you are currently living with the girl you hope to someday marry. Maybe you can begin to see why I chickened out from taking the direct approach.

Plan B involved subtly dropping a reference or two to my girlfriend into the conversation, and then gradually drifting out of that conversation and into one with the history professor, or whichever other person happened to be convenient. This was not exactly an easy thing to do either, but I knew it was the best way I was going to find. As much as I knew I had to drop Gwen on Renee's head, I found myself putting it off. Once Gwen landed, I would never see the same look in Renee's eyes again. I found myself delaying, wishing for one more minute. I knew that look had to go to where I would never find it again, and I just wanted to say goodbye slowly. As bad as we fragile humans need to be loved, it seems a shame sometimes that we can't hold a second layer of love in reserve, in case the first one should ever wear thin. But love is like vacation time to a temp; it just does not accrue. If you are serious about one love, you just can't have a backup waiting in the wings.

I held Gwen back as long as I dared, but when I saw them setting up the bar for a DJ, I knew my time had run out. I saw the whole scenario play out in my mind's eye. Had I been single, it

79

would have been a dream. As it was, it was a nightmare. Renee would turn out to be one of those adorably free spirited girls who grabs a guy and drags him out to dance at the first sound of music. Before long, they would play a slow song, and that only meant touching. As the song went on, the touching would become more and more akin to holding. Two faces would be closer than they had a natural right to be. Pairs of eyes would find each other, and . . .

I convulsed in my seat as I shook the image out of my head. I had to do what I had to do before the DJ surrounded me with quicksand. As casually as I could, I dropped Gwen into the conversation. I felt both, relieved and horribly guilty, when it was done. I swear, I watched a fire truck roll up behind Renee's eyes. Tiny little firemen piled out, unhooked their hose, and sprayed cold, cold water onto the fire there until it was nothing but a lump of black coal. Then one or the other, or both of us, looked away. I think we were both afraid that some of that water would leak out of her eyes. I was never so downhearted at having disappointing someone I had known for such a brief time. I bit my lip to keep a frog from jumping into my throat.

We had to let it go as gracefully as we could. This grace we strove for by turning our backs to each other. I struck up a conversation with the history professor in my corner, while Renee turned to the head of the math department. I can't tell you one word of what was said between myself and the professor in my corner. I was completely focused on feeling guilty about how I had taken Renee up to the cliffs and pushed her off. Besides that, I was trying to covertly listen to the tone of Renee's voice as she talked to the math guy.

I couldn't hear much of Renee's speech. The math professor was much louder, so I heard mostly his end of the conversation, though even many of his words dropped out. All that I was really able to determine was that he seemed very happy to be the object of her attention, and that he used the speech patterns of someone closer to 20 years old than of someone decades older than that. It didn't take long for him to buy her a drink.

The DJ started to play. The blast of music wakened me to the fact that I should call Gwen to let her know why I wasn't home yet. I excused myself from the table to find a quieter spot. I told Gwen where I was, and that I'd be home as soon as I could say my goodbyes. It felt good to hear her voice. I looked forward to going home to her.

When I got back to the table, Renee and the head of the math department were gone. An empty glass marked the place where each of them had been. It didn't take long to find them, as they were among the very few early dancers on the floor. After the mess I had caused, it was only right that I wait for them to return so that I could say a civil goodbye to Renee.

The math professor smiled at Renee as if it were Christmas, 1968, and she were a GI Joe he'd found under the tree. Every so often he would lean over and say something into her ear. She'd nod or make some gesture of understanding, and he'd smile even brighter, as if there were a GI Joe jeep under there too. I began to feel like Mr. Math was trying to feel young again in more ways than I had first imagined.

To my chagrin, they stayed on the floor to dance through a second song. I was tempted to just leave without saying goodbye, but something made me stay. Whether it was just a morbid sort of curiosity, or a real concern for Renee that made me stay, I can't really say. I was a bit taken aback by the lengths that Renee had gone to humor him. She couldn't really be interested in him. I mean, close up, he really was not a handsome man, and it was ridiculous how he was trying to act like a college kid.

Finally, they stopped dancing. When they came back to the table, I could say my obligatory goodbye and go home. The problem was, they didn't come back to our table. Instead, they slipped into a cozy little booth near the dance floor. Sly old Mr.

Math slid his grandpa ass in on the same side of the table as Renee. He bought them another round of drinks, and as they drank, he edged his way up tighter to Renee than her father's older brother should wrap himself around his niece. If Renee noticed this encroachment, she didn't seem to mind. She smiled up into his alarmingly nearby eyes and seemed to encourage him to ply her with sweet talk and alcohol.

I was disgusted and disappointed. How could Renee let this go on? I had just stirred myself to the point of going over there and causing all kinds of trouble for everyone, when the DJ played a slow song. Old Man Math yanked Renee out of their love booth and dragged her onto the floor. He clung to her as if she were a life preserver, lowered down to him by the Coast Guard helicopter of fleeting youth. As they swayed aimlessly, he carefully let his hands drift down her back. I watched in horror, witness to an impending crime I was powerless to prevent.

It's hard to be filled with self-righteous indignation at such a situation when you are man. Your self-righteousness is always vulnerable to your instincts. Dirty Old Math's hand finally came to rest firmly on Renee's behind. I was incensed, partly because it was just wrong for him to take advantage of her in this way, and partly because I had not had a chance to see what a very attractive behind she had before I drove her into his arms. Yes, I still would have let her know about Gwen, but it would have been nice to imagine the full package of what might have been at a time when it still might have been.

So, my righteous indignation may not have been very righteous, and, come to think of it, it may not have been indignation so much as it was envy. Even though Renee could not have me, and I had made that fact plain to her, I still wanted her to want me a little bit before she rushed off into the lecherous arms of Father Time. This, at least, should be my reward for my decision not to be lecherous. Yeah, I know, my reward for being good was waiting for me at home, but a guy should be able to pretend that he suffers from an embarrassment of riches for just a few minutes of his life.

I determined that I would make one honest attempt to break up the travesty I was witnessing before it got out of hand. While I waited for them to sit down again, everyone else at my table, being sensible people, went home to their families, or their cats. I would have appeared downright pitiful if Renee had happened to look over at our table to see me sitting alone, staring at her and her new beau. But she didn't look my way; she didn't look at anything past the picture of Dorian Grey, in whose rotting arms she was held.

When they finally sat down again, I approached their booth boldly. "Hey Renee," I said. "Hey Renee," I said louder, to draw her attention away from him. She looked up like she didn't know me. Her glassy eyes assured me that he wasn't buying her Shirley Temples.

"What?" There was a coldness, an anger, and an echo of hurt in her tone. It hurt me too.

"I'm heading out, and I thought you might need a ride."

Old Math smiled up at me the whole time with his long, sharp teeth. It was the smile of someone who is politely making it known to you that he would have no compunction about biting the jugular right out of your neck.

"I drove here," Renee told me as the waitress set down another round for them.

"I know. But you've had several drinks. I thought you might not want to try and drive tonight."

"I'll see that she gets home safe," Old Math-face butted in. I swear, the grinning old bastard licked his lips.

Renee set her hazy-dreamy eyes upon his grizzly profile. "Dan will take me home," she echoed. The way she said his first name, like it shouldn't be preceded by the word uncle, made him beam with the glee of a weasel who has tunneled under the garden fence of all that is forbidden. That's when I was sure that he was married. Whether his wife were at home, reading bedtime stories to their six children, or out at a different bar, making a play for an adventurous frat boy, I could not say. But I knew to the depths of certainty that she was somewhere.

"That's very kind of him," I said to Renee. "But it's really no problem for me to drop you off on my way."

If her eyes told the truth, she was now quite drunk. "I'm staying right here," she said.

"You sure?"

She answered me by talking to him. "Come on Danny, let's dance." She nudged him out of the booth.

"All right. I'll see you around," I said. As they began to dance, Dan leered his victory at me. He began the dance by slapping both of his boney hands onto her behind as if he owned it.

I walked toward the front door of the bar, but I didn't leave. As soon as I was out of their line of sight, I veered away from the exit. I couldn't leave now. Renee was headed for a horrible train wreck, and I was the one who had switched her engine onto the dangerous track. I felt responsible, and I admit it, I felt jealous. Sure, I understood that a pretty girl like Renee attracts guys. She was going to find a guy she liked among all the chaff. She and the lucky winner would get together and end up doing what comes naturally. That, I could live with. But it shouldn't be like this.

This was not that special guy. This was a dirty old man, thirsting for a quick dip in the fountain of youth, and taking advantage of a laudanum mixture of hurt feelings and liquor. This would always be a regret for Renee, just as knowing that I had caused it would always be a regret for me. It had been stupid and irresponsible of me to flirt so readily with her. Nothing good would ever have come of it, but something terrible had. I could not leave while there was still some small chance of preventing the wreck.

I found a quiet spot and called Gwen. I told her that I had to take some time and have a couple of glasses of water before I drove home, just to be on the safe side. That bought me a little more time, but I hardly knew what to do with it. I ordered myself a soda pop and found a spot where I could see without being seen. The hard part was coming up with a plan to get Renee out of there. The harder part was having to sit there and watch the runaway train, racing toward the break in the track.

No matter how responsible you may feel for pushing somebody down the wrong track, there comes a point when you've just got to let them go. Even if the path Renee was on right now were a reaction to my behavior, she was an adult, and I couldn't make her see reason. This was the conclusion I came to when they started to make out. My gut reaction was to go grab them each by the head and pry their faces apart, but I finally wised up and realized that my presence just added fuel to fire of whatever they thought they were doing. Maybe if she didn't feel me hovering around, humiliating her more tender emotions, Renee could check her less innocent emotions long enough to step back and take a good look at where she was putting her tongue. That was really the only hope left for her.

I turned my back to the carnage and went out. In the parking lot her car was next to mine. It made me feel lonely to see her empty car there. The last time she had been in that car, she'd been my friend. She'd been a bright, beautiful woman. She'd had good judgment, sound values, and virtue. Or maybe that had all just been how I'd wanted her to be. It didn't matter, because perception is reality. The Renee I remembered had been real to me, but never would be again. Worst of all, I knew that I was looking at the car of someone who *used to be* my friend.

I held Gwen tight in my arms when I got home and gave

her a long, hard kiss. She attributed it my being a little buzzed. I'd never been more sober in my life. It wasn't alcohol; it was relief. Even if it took me a little longer than it should have to get around to it, I had eventually done right by Gwen, and in so doing, had done right by myself. I would never again have that hypnotizing, giddy freshness of emerging new love with Gwen. I reckoned that I could live with that. It was a small price to pay for not having to guess at what was real about her. I had seen Gwen endure trials, and I knew her mettle. In the end, I'd rather be sure than giddy.

I cuddled up close to Gwen in bed that night, relieved at the bullet I had dodged. If huge mistakes were being made that night, at least I wasn't the person making them. That was the good news; it made no sense to dwell upon anything else. I was in bed with the woman I wanted to wake up next to. Who other people woke up next to was their own business.

I didn't hear from Renee after that night. In the back of my mind, I hoped she had come to her senses before it was too late, but I had to concentrate on keeping my own life on track. I was back to working my way through the daily quagmire of Steve and Marge Meko, and did not have much time for considering mistakes that had nothing to do with basic arithmetic and alphabetic filing.

I thought about trying to talk to Renee once or twice, but then I didn't know what I would say. I resigned myself to the fact that I might never speak to her again, and silently wished her good luck. She might have been a very good friend, and in a different world, who knows what she could have turned into. But we can only live in one world, and I had to choose how to make that world the best that I could for myself, so I let her go to her own world in peace.

I still felt a little guilty when I recalled that night. I felt like I had chased Renee to the wolves. Worse yet, I felt that I had somehow cheated on Gwen by so carelessly flirting up Renee. As time passed I learned something, and then I was able to let up on myself. I learned that I didn't believe love was as cut and dried as I had wanted to believe it was. I had wanted to fall for the fairy tale that there is one special person in the world for everyone. Now, I know I don't believe that any more. There are so many people in this world. If only one in a million have the potential to be something special to you, well that still leaves quite a handful. God knows there are enough women to be attracted to out there; any particular guy is only going to strike sparks with just one of them? The only way to believe that is to do what I had been doing, not thinking about it.

When the whole theory that I'd embraced, without thinking, got thrown up into my face, it didn't hold up very well. The fact is, if I'd met Renee before Gwen, I'd have gone in hard for her. And it wasn't as if I even had to look to find somebody like that. It just snuck up on me. Everybody likes the feeling of falling for someone new. So what do you do about that when you've already got somebody old? I guess you either keep trading for that next temporary rush, or you develop some self-discipline. Beating yourself up doesn't seem to help.

9.
Waxing Moon, Gawking Mother

Well, just when things really stink at work, and I'm trying to keep perspective by realizing how good I've got it in my personal life, tragedy strikes my personal life. Gwen's parents relented; they will allow my likeness to be represented on their Christmas card this year. That, in and of itself, is not the tragedy. It's not the endowment from Heaven that Gwen's parents seem to think it is, but it's not the tragedy. It's only the invitation to tragedy. Look, I have no problem with Gwen's parents, but they are so different from me, in so many ways, that any circumstance causing our paths to cross foments a breeding ground for tragedy.

I'm not sure why they changed their minds. My character has certainly not improved since they've known me. I'm still pretty much a classic ne'er-do-well who somehow managed to get my dubious hooks into their daughter. Maybe it's some master scheme to extract her from the orbit of my cult of personality. It's anybody's guess.

Though I can't imagine why this change in official Goldblatt family policy was made, I can readily picture *how* it was made. I see Doug and Lydia Goldblatt sitting under a remarkably tasteful lamp, loaded with a 100 watt bulb, painstakingly making out a list of pros and cons of letting Gary into the picture. They do the cons first, because they come to mind so easily. It would be a shame to let those valuable cons slip away into the ether before they could be gotten down in ink. The pros are not so easy. Doug chews the end of the pen as they both rack their brains. The funny thing about the pros, when they do finally come, is that they all have Gwen's name attached to them; the cons all start with Gary, or later, when Mr. Goldblatt's writing hand gets tired, simply "he."

After they've given themselves headaches trying to scratch up a few pros, Doug sets down his pen and they look over the list. There are many times more Garys than there are Gwens, but then one Gwen is worth a whole handful of Garys, so the voting could be close. And voting there is to be. They start with a secret ballot, the two of them, sitting poker-faced across the table from one another. They each scribble a simple yes or no on a piece of paper, fold it, and slide it to the middle. Lydia, the official Goldblatt family clerk, unfolds the papers in their turn and announces the ballot. The first ballot takes the assembly (Mr. Goldblatt) by surprise. "Yes," Mrs. Goldblatt dispassionately reads.

Mr. Goldblatt does some quick math in his head and comes to the reassuring conclusion that this first round of voting will end in stalemate. As he breathes relief, Mrs. Goldblatt unfolds the second slip of paper and declares it a "No." At this, the process begins again. They carefully look over the list of pros and cons as Mrs. Goldblatt prepares the second ballot. This vote, and the three succeeding, are doomed to impasse. As the two sides begin to stare each other down, somebody suggests that the floor be opened to debate.

Doug is steadfast in his stand on principle. The Christmas card is reserved for members of the Goldblatt family, not for bounders who are intent on leading their daughter astray. This Gary Gray character is not even engaged to Gwen. The only commitment he has made to her involves luring her into his, let's just say, lair. Georgia didn't get onto the Christmas card until she and Dale were engaged. Never mind that Georgia was a good girl who didn't coax Dale into shacking up with her before they were married. If they let that Gary Gray into the picture, it would just encourage his kind of behavior.

89

Lydia does not quarrel with Doug's reasoning. The logic behind his argument is unassailable. But Lydia misses her daughter. "I have no more use for that Gary Gray than you do," she assures her husband, "but I'm tired of being on the outs with Gwen." The estrangement has taken its toll on Lydia, and if putting that Gary Gray's ugly mug on the Christmas card is the price she has to pay to win her little girl back, it's come time to pay it. Lydia's position is materially strengthened by the way her eyes get all watery when she talks about her baby girl.

At the end of the debate period, Mr. Goldblatt proposes a motion that the next vote be by show of hands. This is highly irregular, but Mrs. Goldblatt, in her emotional condition, is unprepared to fight for convention. The motion passes. There is nothing left but to bring forward the next round of voting on the issue of whether that Gary Gray should be allowed into the family Christmas card photo, to be distributed during the forthcoming holiday season. "All in favor," Lydia solicits as she leads by example with her hand raised high.

Mr. Goldblatt rolls his eyes and stretches his lips around his front teeth. What he is about to do is a great concession for him. He can't do it easily, and he won't do it eagerly. Still, it must be done. He sighs. For his dear wife, for his misled daughter, and in spite of that Gary Gray, Mr. Goldblatt's forearm begins to twitch. It takes all of his strength to lift that long ton of bricks attached to his shoulder, but he does it, slowly and painfully. At last, there are two people in the room with hands raised. The issue is settled. Lydia comes around the table to give her husband a big hug. She's getting her baby girl back. Tomorrow, after the joy has had time to settle, the Goldblatt's will sit down to the onerous task of figuring out how to deal with that Gary Gray.

Though there are plenty of reasons why I would have been content to leave things as they were regarding the Christmas card photo, the look on Gwen's face when she got the news made me glad for the change in policy. It was a kind of beaming glow you don't get to see in a person every day, the kind of parade that a man with any heart in his body can't bring himself to rain upon. Gwen had finally gotten her family back, and it was not at all becoming of me to forget that I was the reason she had lost them in the first place. It made me realize how much she had really given up for me, and knowing that was worth smiling for the camera.

This year, the annual Christmas card photo was to be taken in July instead of October. Rather than fake a winter scene as they usually did, the Goldblatts decided that they would take the picture at their cottage on Lake Victorian Sensibilities at the height of summer. There was to be no attempt at winterizing the scene at all. The only things that would be Christmasy in the least were the pine trees and the insulated Santa Claus caps that Mrs. Goldblatt insisted everyone wear. I think the theme of the card was to be something like this: NOW THAT IT'S THE MIDDLE OF COLD WINTER, REMEMBER WHAT A PLEASANT SUMMER JUST PASSED? IN CASE YOU DON'T, LET US TAUNT YOU BY SMILING INCESSANTLY AT YOU FROM THE MIDST OF OUR BALMY SUMMER IDYLL, AS YOU PUT ON YOUR DIRTY BOOTS IN PREPARATION FOR ANOTHER FORLORN ATTEMPT AT GETTING YOUR CAR WITH ITS FROZEN BATTERY STARTED. That may not be it exactly, but I'm pretty sure it was something along those lines. The whole idea of it made me regret that I would not be there when my dad got his Christmas card from the Goldblatts. My dad is the king of dirty, inadequately insulated boots and frozen car batteries. Then again, I *would* be there with him, in my comfy summer spirit, smiling at him from carefree July. Of all the cards on display atop my mom's special Christmas card display table, it would be the only one that had to be taped back together. During the moments when I began to panic and regret my willingness to be included in the photo, this one thought kept me firm in my resolve to don the Santa hat among the pines.

The drive up to Lake Victorian Sensibilities was noteworthy only for the number of times we got lost trying to navigate the spider web of dirt roads that give the lake region its teen horror film charm. Driving around lost brought out the true nature of our respective genders. Gwen kept insisting that I stop and ask directions. I absolutely refused to do any such thing, stuck in my stubborn man-pride, and my disbelief that the squirrels and chipmunks could offer any meaningful assistance.

Gwen got more and more annoyed at my refusal to ask directions, and I got more and more annoyed by the fact that she had been to her parents' cottage many times, and still could not get us close. A series of random objects would seem familiar enough to convince her that we were on the right track. This would immediately be followed by a series of random objects that were so unfamiliar as to convince her that I had somehow gotten us further away from the goal than ever. It didn't matter that I had not altered our course in the least since we were almost there.

Gwen was threatening to get out and walk, and I was threatening to let her, when the cottage sprang up before us. I had expected a small, rustic-looking building, fashioned of hewn logs, and maybe even an outhouse. What I saw was a house far more palatial than my primary residence would ever be. The entire time I had imagined myself to be lost deep in the primeval forest, there had been a row of such mansions just out of sight. They ringed the lake, and if we had been on the right road, I would have been able to stare in awe at them, one after another, as we made the quick trip along the shore.

Instead of an outhouse the place had three full baths on its two spacious levels. It had all the amenities of home, including cable TV, and though it was a weekend retreat, it was kept up much more fastidiously than our apartment. I considered it a victory for me, and my entire class of people, when I smelled the faint mustiness that is inherent in a house in the woods by a lake. They couldn't sanitize that musty odor completely out of their perfect world, could they?

Of the things it is within the power of humans to do something about, I found only two minor flaws in the whole cottage. Those two flaws were in a section of the house to which guests would not normally go, and it was only an unforeseen circumstance that sent me to them. I wish I had never discovered those flaws, as they caused me a great deal of grief. I wish that I could remember the Goldblatt's summer cottage as inhumanly perfect, but I will never be able to imagine that again. I'm getting ahead of myself, though; I will get to the flaws in the cottage in good time.

My reception at the cottage was, if not warm, polite. I half wished that Doug and Lydia would go ahead and make a full airing of their grievances against me at the start, rather than staring silent judgment at me for a full second before opening their mouths to speak to me. I don't mean just the first time; I mean every time one of them asked me a polite question about the state of my affairs. I knew exactly what was foremost in their minds, simply because they would not come near it in conversation. Nothing they asked me had anything to do with my intentions toward their daughter. When they spoke to me about my doings, it was almost as if I were a lonesome traveler who had stopped for the night and offered up two guineas for lodgings. Though Gwen sat beside me, you would have guessed that they thought me a stranger to her.

Gwen noticed this phenomenon as well, and tried to combat it by interposing statements that featured the word "we." She made a point to say things like, "We are thinking about getting a puppy." I didn't know that we were thinking about getting a puppy, and probably, we weren't, but it was a sentence that started with "we,' and that, I suppose, was the important thing.

Whenever Gwen made one of these statements, her parents would let slip a short frown, and one or the other of them would say something encouraging, like, "Oh, I see." Then they would proceed to ask me another question on a completely different topic, so that they could wedge Gwen out of my conversational life from a different angle. It developed into quite a battle of wits between Gwen and her parents. I stayed out of it as best I could, because I don't have wits to spare on a war that is destined to end in stalemate.

If the Goldblatts would like Gwen to throw me back so that she might catch a fish with bigger prospects, which I suspect they do, they sure have their strategy all fouled up. Gwen and I were not very happy with each other when we first arrived at the cottage, blaming each other for getting lost. Doug and Lydia did a marvelous job, in spite of themselves, of bringing me back into Gwen's good graces, by supplying, not one, but two people who were even more annoying to her than I was that day. Their leading questions led her right back to my side and let her forget all about the vexatious ass I had been earlier. Ironically, my parents think Gwen is the best thing since sliced bread, which is the only real threat to our relationship.

Gwen and I were assigned to beds, sized appropriately for toddlers, in different rooms. In a concession to habits of modern youth, the rooms were allowed to be adjacent. The beds were, no doubt, the same ones that Gwen and Dale had used when the family came to spend time at the lake 20 years ago. Dale and Georgia were accommodated in the guest bedroom, where married folks were allowed to cuddle, and straighten out their legs all they wished.

By lying diagonally, and arching my body, I could get everything except my feet onto the mattress. Remarkably, I was able to fall to sleep several times. Each of these naps was interrupted by the cold, wet touch of a German Wirehaired

Pointer's nose against the soles of my feet. Rex, frustrated by the dearth of female, canine companionship on the lake, took solace in the odor of my feet, which, judging from the excitement they brought to Rex, smell very much like a bitch in heat.

When the big picture-taking day dawned, I was pretty tired. At dawn Doug and Lydia went about waking up the house, so that none of us could reproach ourselves for having wasted any part of another glorious day on the lake. Apparently, the Goldblatts believe that going into the woods for the weekend makes you a pioneer, or somebody who should act like one. This means getting up at an ungodly hour in order to give yourself plenty daylight, in case you have a full day of blazing a trail through the wilderness, or evading bears and Indians, to do.

This was especially unfortunate for me, as Rex had given up that my feet would ever return his affections about an hour before, and I had wedged myself into a position from which none of me dangled, so that I could finally get some sleep. But you know what they say: when in Rome, do a lot of senseless, crazy shit, just because the natives don't know any better. So, I went downstairs and had a cup of coffee. Everybody else filled up on Lydia's home-cooked breakfast, but I could hardly swallow coffee at that hour, let alone chew food. I think it may have hurt Lydia's feelings that I stayed away from her hot cakes, but I did my best to explain my dilemma, when I was not nodding off mid-sentence.

I knew I was going to fall asleep again if I didn't get up and do something, so I got the great idea to take Gwen on a canoe trip. That went okay for a couple of hours, until Gwen began to get seasick and I got pretty tired of all that paddling. The Goldblatts have a little motor boat, but we weren't allowed to use that because it was "just for emergencies." I wonder, if we had capsized the canoe and were clinging to it for dear life, would that have been enough of an emergency to make them dust off the outboard and rescue us? As long as Gwen were clinging there with me, I guess it probably would have been enough.

By the Grace of God, we did not flip the canoe. We only struggled against a stiff headwind, as Gwen got greener and greener. Somehow, she managed to avoid throwing up, but at the expense of bursting into tears. Only through the supreme power of her will did she find the strength, through bitter tears and nausea, to vehemently implore me to paddle faster while she rested her head in her folded arms.

By the time we made landfall, Gwen was pretty upset: half at me, for taking her so far out on the lake and then being so slow to bring her back; half at the elements for turning so rough on her; and half at herself, for finding it so easy to blame me and the elements. Gwen is a very passionate woman; when she gets riled, she can become up to 50 percent more upset than the average person. At that level, there was nothing for me to do but help her out of the canoe and then leave her alone.

All that single-handed paddling wore me out. I went inside and sat on the couch, for about a second. Within the next second, I was lying on the couch. By the third second, I was asleep on the couch. It was a sound sleep, with nary a nightmare about futile canoe paddling or impending vomit. It was sweet oblivion.

Gwen shook me awake. She looked much better than when she had climbed out of the canoe. In fact she looked quite beautiful. She was all made up, which seemed somewhat incongruous with a Saturday afternoon at the lake, until she reminded me that it was almost time for the Christmas card photo. As her father would abide no delays in his photo shoot schedule, she encouraged me to go quickly to the shower, unless I wanted to appear in the picture like I had just returned from a hard life at sea and fallen asleep on the couch for three hours.

As it happened, Dale and Georgia were running a little behind as well. Consequently, both of the guest bathrooms were occupied. I was perfectly prepared to wait it out and grab a few more winks, but then Doug came upon us. Doug was not the man to compromise his strict Christmas-card-picture-taking schedule, which is just what would have happened if I had my druthers. Nor did Doug take kindly to the idea of having his picture tainted by an unwashed ragamuffin, the likes of my current self. It was bad enough he had to have a washed ragamuffin, such as I was at my best. An unwashed ragamuffin was out of the question.

Caught between falling behind schedule and taking me dirty, Doug made what must have been a horribly distasteful decision. He sent me to the master bath for my shower. His eyelid may have twitched involuntarily as he did it, but he was nonetheless resolved.

I cut through the master bedroom, with its prim and polished, parental decor, as quickly as I could. I wished to be in the place where Doug and Lydia shared their bed as briefly as possible. I slipped into the master bath like a creeping housebreaker, trying to convince the very walls of the place that they had not seen me. I closed the bathroom door behind me, but it failed to latch and swung open again. I jiggled the knob and closed it again. This time it stayed shut.

Recall that I mentioned that I found only two flaws in the entire cottage. I had just encountered the first. The second became apparent after I had stripped and gotten into the shower. As I pulled the curtain closed behind me at the head of the shower, it left a gap at the other end. I tugged the curtain back and forth, trying to get it to cover the entire length of its rod, but the curtain would not reach from one wall to the other. Anticipating the scandal that would be caused by leaving a puddle of shower water on the pristine bathroom floor, I resolved to stand as close under the showerhead as I could and to be extra careful of excess splatter.

The Goldblatts are partial to those flower-scented, moisturizing bars of soap. I despise that kind of soap, mostly

97

because it has that dish soap quality that makes you feel greasy after having washed with it. I never feel clean after showering with this kind of soap. Rather, I feel like I have locked in the dirt on my body under a protective sheen of waterproof oil. But since the moisturizing soap was the only bar in the shower, and I had already lathered up my head with a shampoo that promised to make my hair perky, it was oily soap or nothing.

I was soon reminded that there is another reason why I don't like moisturizing soaps: they are near impossible for me to hang onto with wet hands. I was futilely trying to get the soap to lather when it squirted out of my hand. It popped out through the top of my grasp, flew upward for a little ways, then started to fall. Being a quick-witted fellow, I made a swipe to try and catch it.

I got my hand on the soap, but I didn't catch it; I merely batted it away. It should have hit the shower curtain and fallen at my feet. This is where flaw number two in the cottage came into play. The batted soap, sped through the gap between the abbreviated shower curtain and the wall. It glanced off the bathroom door and rebounded, skidding across the floor and disappearing behind the toilet.

I should have just rinsed the perky shampoo out of my hair and called it good. That would have been the thinking man's course of action. But, it turns out, I can't think and take a shower at the same time. I didn't know that I have a resolve for finishing a shower, once begun, but apparently, I do. I did not for a second consider any course short of retrieving the wayward soap and finishing the job.

I stepped out from under the water and tried to let as much drip off of me before exiting the shower. Again, the thinking man might have reached for his towel, and perhaps even wrapped it about himself before stepping out onto the bathroom floor. At the time, however, it did not even occur to me that a man's towel could be accessed at any time prior to completion of both the soaping and rinsing processes of the shower. I am a man who believes in the strict order of things, and the strict order of things will very likely kill me in the end.

I stepped out onto the floor on tip-toe, as if that would minimize the dripping. I was so focused on not dripping that I hardly noticed my hip brushing the door. The bathroom was pretty narrow, with the toilet on the end away from the door, so as I scanned for the runaway soap, my back was to the door. The soap was not difficult to spot, though it proved much harder to reach.

I was in full bend, at the point of getting my fingers around the soap, when I began to realize that things were not as I imagined them to be. I heard Lydia's voice. That she was coming toward the master bedroom I could tell by the Doppler effect her voice was creating as she neared. The odd thing was that her voice was not muffled at all by the bathroom door. The odder thing was that this oddity had no effect upon my consciousness. I was focused upon the soap, which merely required a little scoot with my middle finger before I could get it within my grasp.

Lydia's voice grew louder, like the piercing whistle of an onrushing train. I began to hear her words. "Doug, you'd better hurry up in there if you're going to keep your sched . . ." Then there was a loud gasp. The gasp seemed so close that I thought I could feel the breeze of it evaporating water from my skin. It was just enough stimulus to make me turn my head.

Where the door should have been was only wide open doorway. A couple of feet beyond stood the bolt upright Lydia, both hands cupped over her mouth, eyes so paralyzed with horror that they could not pull themselves from my shame. Doug would certainly never accept me now, as this would make the second Goldblatt girl that I had robbed of her innocence.

If you think there was nothing I could do to make matters worse, you'd be wrong. I had turned my head so lazily that I had not even bothered to straighten myself into an upright position.

Instead, I had just craned my neck so that I could look back over my shoulder. Now, as Lydia gazed her horror at me, and I gazed my horror back at her, I was in too much shock to stand up and spring behind the protective cover of the transparent shower curtain. Rather, I froze, bent over and looking back, like a cow keeping a wary eye out for a soft-stepping bull.

It took precious, long seconds for me to realize that I was not showing Lydia my best side, though both ends of me felt about the same at the moment. Only then did I properly panic by leaping into the shower and pulling the clear curtain closed behind me. This changed my vulnerable position in that it gave Lydia a chance to see that I was more bull than cow.

Now that Lydia had seen me from front and back, I gave her an action pose as I stretched myself out of the shower and grabbed for my towel. Somehow, the act of wrapping the towel around me snapped her out of her trance. I feared she would faint, but she merely turned, on wobbly legs, and left. Meanwhile I stood under the water, wrapped in a soaked towel. I turned the water as hot as I could bear and tried to burn the dirtiness off my soul. The soap was still on the floor behind the toilet, but that didn't matter. It was greasy soap that would just lacquer the dirtiness onto my soul.

It is not easy to hold a door closed and wring out a soaked towel all at the same time, yet this is just what I was doing when someone knocked at the bathroom door. This sudden shock rattled me to the point where I imagined that Doug had come to finish me off with his electric, turkey-carving knife. I don't know if I were more alarmed by that possibility or by the fact that I was still stark naked. If Lydia were returning for her well-deserved apology, I was in no position to mitigate the damages.

"Gary? What are you doing in there? Dad's all ready to go." It was Gwen's voice. I relaxed my white-knuckled grip on the door knob.

100

"Are you alone?" I asked.

"Yes, I'm alone." Her tone added an unspoken, "Duh!"

I ignored the tone. "Completely alone?"

"Of course, completely. Who would I bring to get you out of the bathroom?"

"Okay, come in."

I'd never been ashamed to have Gwen see me naked before, but now a second full wave of dirtiness swept over me. I wrapped my drenched towel around my mid-section and stared at her with the repentant eyes of a very naughty boy.

"Why is your towel soaking wet?" she asked my naughtiness.

I opened my mouth as if I had some explanation, but the facts of the matter swamped my brain. "I have no idea," I told her, and at that moment there was no truer answer in the world.

"Wait here," she sighed. She came back with a dry towel, which made me love her more than ever, because wet skin and fresh memories were making me shiver. She took me back to my toddler room and helped me dress; I never needed more help in my life.

Gwen dragged me out to the lakefront photo shoot just in time to keep Doug's impatience from boiling over. As it was, he was very business-like as he arranged us into our places. Somebody pushed a Santa cap onto my head as Doug fit me into my spot. At one point, my eyes met Lydia's, and she nearly went down in a swoon. I was still in quite a daze myself, so I did not resist when a determined set of hands positioned me on my knees with Rex, in front. Gwen tried to get me back up with the humans, but I somehow convinced her that I was perfectly fine with Rex. There was little chance of more eye contact with Lydia from this level, and nothing else mattered. It was the perfect spot, as far as I was concerned. Besides, Rex and I were old friends from the night before. At least Rex and I hadn't done anything together that would make us pass out at the sight of each other.

I have no recollection of how long I stayed on the ground with Rex. I just knelt and stared into the camera lens as Doug flitted about making everything perfect. I remember Doug marching back and forth between the tripod and the family, and I remember him commanding everyone to smile, but I don't think I smiled. I think I just stared. Undoubtedly, I will look inconsolable when the card comes out. The best case scenario is that I will merely appear to be stoned out of my mind. Either way, it's another reason to look forward to the holidays.

We were supposed to stay over another night at the lake, but I begged Gwen to go home early. I told her I didn't feel well; the tiny bed was making me sore; I had lots to do in the morning at home. I came up with every excuse to head home at night, except for the one that went: "Your mom saw me naked—front and back—and now I can't bear to face her again." Yet that was the true reason I wanted to go home so badly. I wanted to go and sit in the tub for a few hours and scrub the shame off me. I couldn't do that at the cottage because I was afraid to undress. Besides that, the soap was useless, and as far as I knew, still hiding behind the toilet.

Gwen's bed wasn't any more comfortable than mine was, and I think that's the reason she finally gave in and agreed to go home that night. The Goldblatts hugged their daughter goodbye. Lydia waved vaguely at me while staring at her feet. Doug gave me a ritual handshake that did not indicate any warming of his feelings for me, but also assured me that Lydia had not let him in on our shameful secret. I got us out of there a soon as I could, as I did not know how long Lydia could carry the awful burden of scandal all by herself.

It was the end of a long day. Gwen and I didn't talk much on the ride home. I found myself drifting inward. I was already dreading the day when the Christmas card arrived. I tried to imagine some miracle by which the card would never get to us, but even a miracle would not hold up against Gwen's certain eagerness to see the picture that finally had both her and me in it. The card would come, and Gwen would open it the moment it did.

I could see it so vividly in the windshield as I drove through the night. Gwen, like anybody else, would check out her own image first. She would look cute, like she always did in photos. Next, she would move to the image of my face. She would make a joke about how empty my stare appeared, though the joke would not fully mask her disappointment that I did not look very handsome in this particular photo. Then she would move her eyes over the faces of her family. She would make an offhand comment here and there until she got to her mother. Then she would comment upon how similarly empty her mother's countenance was to mine.

Gwen's a really sharp woman, but in my guilty reverie I gave her supernatural powers of deduction. "Why do you and my mom have the same vacant look on your faces?" the Gwen in my head asked. "What went on that day? Did my mom see you naked?"

"Why do you say that?" the me in my head protested. "What would make you say such a thing?"

"It's as plain as the look on her face," my imagined, super-sleuthing girlfriend explained. "She looks like she's seen a ghost, and we both know how pale-white your bony little butt is. Meanwhile, you also look as if you've seen a ghost; she must have appeared truly ghostly to you, bathed in the light of that bright-white moon of yours. It's a simple matter of connecting the dots. Would you like to confess now?"

I shook off the drama playing in my head and reminded myself that it had all been a terrible accident. At least, as far as I knew, it had been an accident. There was no way that I could ever be absolutely sure that Lydia had not come to bask in the glow of

103

my special moonlight on purpose. I shuddered so violently that the car actually swerved.

Gwen rolled out of her doze. "What's going on? You all right?"

"Your mom saw me naked." Gwen hadn't said that, so it must have been me. Funny, I hadn't anticipated saying it, and yet I clearly heard it said, in a male voice.

"What?"

"You'd probably figure it out anyway, when you saw the Christmas card."

"What the hell are you talking about, Gary?"

"It was an accident, I think."

"Wait. Hold on a second. My mom saw you naked?"

"Yes."

"When?"

"Today."

"When, today?"

"When I was taking a shower in your parents' bathroom."

"How?"

"Like I said, I think it was an accident."

"Excuse me? My mom sees you naked in the shower, and all you have is a *theory* that it *might* have been an accident?"

"I wouldn't call it a *theory*. I'd say it was more of a *conclusion* that it almost *certainly* was an accident."

"*Almost* certainly? Let's break this down a little. Are you *completely* certain it was an accident on *your* part?"

"Oh yeah, opening that bathroom door was completely accidental."

"You opened the door? Why the hell would you open the door while you were taking a shower?"

"I wasn't in the shower. I got out."

"And the first thing a normal person does when they step out of the shower is throw open the bathroom door for the viewing

104

pleasure of passersby."

"I wasn't trying to open the door," I protested. "I dropped the soap behind the toilet and I got out of the shower to go get it."

"Wait. You dropped the soap, in the shower, and it somehow managed to land behind the toilet?"

"Not exactly. See, I dropped it, and then kind of batted it, and it flew out behind the toilet."

"And you were playing shuttlecock with the soap, why?" Any other day she would have called the game badminton, like a normal American, but my clever girl quickly grasped how much more humiliating shuttlecock sounded when applied to a naked man.

"I dropped it; I tried to catch it; I swiped it, and it flew off behind the toilet, okay?"

"So, of course, you fling open the door, in case anybody is at hand to help you retrieve it."

"Are you even listening," I huffed. "I told you I wasn't trying to open the door. I don't know how it opened. I may have brushed the door with my hip."

"And your hip's so strong that the door just flew wide open?"

"It didn't fly. It must have kind of swung, quietly. I didn't even know it was open. I wouldn't have bent over like that if I'd known it was open."

"Bent over like what?"

"Bent over like *bent over*. How many ways can you bend over?"

"And that's what mom saw?"

"That's the first thing."

"Oh God! I don't even want to see that. She saw more than that?"

"When I turned around."

"At least that might have left a better impression."

105

"She didn't need to squint, if that's what you mean."

"I'm sure that was a relief to her. It would have been a real imposition on her to have to run downstairs and get her glasses."

"Well, if she wanted her glasses, she was in no big hurry to run and get them."

"What's that mean?"

"Only that she hung around long enough to get a good eyeful."

"Eyeful? I bet she was struck blind by the first sight of you."

"She wasn't looking at me like any blind woman I've ever seen."

"So what are you saying? My mother was checking you out the whole time?"

"I don't know. Maybe mother and daughter have the same taste in men. Maybe your sweet tooth for a scrumptious piece of candy like me runs in the family."

Gwen had no answer for this sterling bit of deduction, mostly because she was choking on her laughter.

"Hey, all I'm saying is, take a good look at the evidence," I insisted.

"Oh yeah, like the way I always coat the soap in butter and lurk around the bathroom waiting for you to drop it?" She was mastering her laughter well enough to mock me now.

"I was wondering why we go through butter so fast."

"Hey, a girl's got to use whatever's handy when she gets that craving to sneak a peek at such a sexy, lily-white ass. You know, we girls like bright, shiny things."

"Well, your mom didn't exactly turn away at the first opportunity."

"Of course not. What woman could turn away from such a beautiful sight. I bet the only reason she left the room at all was to go get her sunglasses. Hey, when the Christmas card comes, you want me to put it up in the bathroom, so you two can relive your special moment?"

It went on like that all the way home. I don't know when Gwen ever laughed so much. She had a great time of busting my balls. It was a little humiliating at first, but that passed quickly. By the time we got home, I was laughing too. I could laugh because Gwen, through her own laughter, had made it all right. She'd taken the trauma out of it and turned it into just another ridiculous episode in the farce that is my life.

I had left the cottage numb, haunted by a terrible secret that I assumed would pursue me endlessly and form barriers between me and Gwen, not to mention her family. By the time we got home, I was laughing at my own embarrassment. It had been an unfortunate accident, and all the barriers were false. Gwen had cut right through to this, and with her humor, had made me see it too. She knew better than to try and soothe me with soft reassurances. She knew me well enough to know that she needed to hold my silly fears up to ridicule. That was the only way somebody like me would see them for what they were. She's good at tough love that way. By the end of the night, everything was okay. That's why I love her so much.

10.
If You Can't Take the Heat, Get Out of the Men's Room

The events leading to my unfortunate mooning of Gwen's mom kicked off a series of occurrences that have forced me to come face to face with a profound, unflattering truth about myself. I have a difficult time navigating bathroom situations. There, I've admitted it, put it right out in the sunlight. I don't know if this character flaw is the result of a compilation of bad experiences, or if the character flaw has been the cause of the bad experiences. I guess it really doesn't matter. I'm doomed to keep upsetting people with my awkward bathroom behavior.

My friend, Len, is pissed at me. Len went to high school with me. He's a grad student in Philosophy here at Appalachian Downslope College. (My crowd is all headed into high-paying fields.) Len called me at work yesterday, wanting to know what my problem was. I happen to have several problems, so I wasn't sure which he was inquiring about. I told him as much.

"Why didn't you say 'hello' to me?" he wanted to know.

"I'm not allowed to say 'hello' when I answer the phone," I told him. "I have to say, 'Appalachian Downslope College, accounting department. Gary speaking.'"

"Not when you answered the phone, Nimrod. Fifteen minutes ago."

I was confused. "Fifteen minutes ago," I explained. "I was in the men's room."

"Exactly. I was in the men's room 15 minutes ago too—the very same men's room you were in. You didn't say 'hi.' You didn't even acknowledge my existence."

"I didn't hear *you* say 'hi,'" I fired back.

"I nodded at you," he said, as if there were some point to that.

"Why didn't you say something?"

"Cause you walked past so fast I didn't have a chance, and I didn't want to chase you around the place. It was the bathroom, after all."

"Exactly."

At some point during our friendship, I should have explained my policy regarding men's rooms to Len. I see now that I never did that, so I am going to make a broadcast statement here and now. My policy on men's rooms is as follows: there are no friends in men's rooms; there are no acquaintances in men's rooms; if I had my way there would be no such thing as men's rooms. There would only be man's rooms. You see, I'm very uncomfortable with the communalization of the business that goes on in such places. I'm old school, a rugged individualist, American. I believe that the business of bathrooms should be limited to one person per four walls at a time. People should do those sorts of things in private, and if possible, in secret.

I don't believe that I have ever said "hello" to anyone in a men's room, except under deep duress. In fact, I try very hard not to recognize anyone I see in a men's room. Eye contact is avoided at all costs. Everyone is a stranger in the men's room, the more unfamiliar the better. Face it, a lot of unpleasant things happen in the men's room. There are smells, and sounds, and God forbid, sights, in the men's room that would not be allowed anywhere else in society. I prefer the rules of outside society to what goes on in the men's room. Much more than needs be true of Las Vegas, I believe that what happens in the men's room should stay in the men's room. Hence, I don't want to know who does it. I don't want to recognize people by their men's room actions. I don't want to know who made my trip to wash my hands so nastily unpleasant, and I don't want them to recognize me as the person who was negatively affected by their moment of constitutional vulnerability.

Knowing my own tendencies, I would most likely keep meticulous track of who left the men's room without washing his hands. I don't want to live like that. I don't want to divide my world into the clean and the unclean any more than the manifestly filthy force me to do. If I don't see your face, I won't know what side you're on when I run into you an hour later, and that's the way I like it. So don't nod at me, because I'm not seeing anything above your shoes.

In fact one of the most traumatic occurrences of my life involved the breeching of my anonymity in a men's room. I was sitting there, minding my own business, when I heard someone enter the next stall. This in itself was disturbing to me, as I really prefer to have a buffer stall in between. Trying very hard to block the sounds from the other side of the partition from my mind, I was coping with the stress pretty well when a voice from over there asked, "Cletus, that you?"

I froze. My mind raced. Who was he talking to? As far as I knew, there was nobody else in the room. He couldn't be talking to me, could he? Nobody else responded. He must be talking to me. What did he expect? An answer? Did he expect me to talk to him through the stall? How could anyone be so contemptible as to expect such an unseemly thing?

"Hey, Cletus?" he asked again. I don't really remember the name of the person he was asking for, but when I think of the kind of men who converse between stalls, I think of Cletus.

By now I was pretty sure he was talking to me, or rather the person he believed to be Cletus, sitting next to him. I wanted very badly to let him know that I was not Cletus, and hopefully, put a quick end to his efforts at inter-staller communication. Yet, I could not make the simplest sound pass my throat. My mouth was dry, my throat paralyzed. They had never been expected to work in this situation before, so why should they be ready now?

Finally, my neighbor became impatient. He banged on the stainless steel between us. "Cletus, dammit, say something!" he bellowed.

The shock of the violent bang nearly sent me sprawling from my perch. Fortunately, I had just barely enough grit to hold my place. Meanwhile, my voice was startled into service. "I'm not Cletus," I said meekly. Even though my statement could hardly have been issued above a whisper, the words seemed to echo through my brain as they bounced off the walls of my cell. I felt dirty and ashamed, as one who has broken a sacred code of silence. I had violated my own dear principle of anonymity, and broken it in the most flagrant manner; I had spoken across the most sacrosanct no-man's land.

"Oh," replied the un-contrite voice from beyond the fallen barrier. "I thought you was Cletus. He's in that one a lot."

I did not respond. Now was the time for action, not words. With a clear purpose, I sped to close out my affairs in that vicinity, for if there were one face I especially did not want to see in the men's room that day, it was the face of the voice that had called me Cletus. Afterward, I took great pains never to return to that particular men's room, for if there were one face that I never wished to risk seeing in the men's room thereafter, it was that of Cletus himself.

Getting back to my phone conversation with my pissed-off friend, Len: he was still upset about the lack of acknowledgement he got from me in the men's room. He seemed to know that it was inappropriate to chase people around the bathroom, but he could not relate this knowledge to my assertion that it was best to leave them alone altogether.

"Tell me this," I asked. "Would you have chased me down if we'd passed in a cafeteria?"

"I wouldn't have had to chase you," he said. "You would have sat down at a table and I would have caught up to you then."

"Well, how did you know I wasn't about to sit down in the men's room?"

"I didn't want to take that chance."

"Neither did I. That's why I don't go scouting out for people I know in the men's room."

"I wasn't scouting out," he protested. "I was just being friendly, which is more than I can say for you."

"Len, do you ever schedule meetings in the men's room?"

"Dude, get real."

"Ever go into the men's room thinking, 'Gee, I sure hope I run into so-and-so in there. Haven't seen him in the toilet in a while.'?"

He snorted at me. "Now you're just being a dick."

"Okay, okay. I can see this is upsetting to you. Tell you what, I'll make it up to you. I'll buy you a beer after work, and we'll put it all behind us. How's that?"

"Well," his tone moderated. "That'd be a step in the right direction. Where?"

"You know that new place down on College Ave.?"

"The sports bar?"

"That's the one."

"Okay."

"Yeah, meet me in the men's room of that place at six."

That's when he hung up on me. He'll get over it.

112

11.
Marge Meko Commands That I Sleep With the Fishes

Through all the time that I was discovering various irregularities in the way the accounting department at Appalachian Downslope College did business, I kept thinking to myself, "Boy, I sure would like to meet the auditor who lets this shit just slide on by every year." That was before I met him. I should have known to be more careful about what I wished for.

He sauntered into the office Monday morning with the air of a war hero, back when people liked war heroes, coming home to embrace the thanks and praise due him for single-handedly wiping out that Nazi tank battalion. Marge Meko's eyes lit up when she saw him, just as if he'd really dealt the Third Reich a death blow. That's what I thought at the time, but now I know that Marge Meko was greeting the arrival of an entire squadron of cavalry, riding in to rid her of the torment caused by a circling band of one little Indian: me.

Bernie Timpt had the same dark, shifty eyes as Marge Meko. The resemblance began there, and spread itself outward over his unpleasant face and then his entire frumpy body. His face—full of bulbous features, from his nose to his cheeks, and even his brow—so well matched that of Marge Meko that they easily could have been siblings. Much to my relief, I later learned that they were not siblings; they were nothing more prejudicial to the interests of objective oversight than first cousins.

113

Marge Meko rushed to give him a hug, and for that brief moment I pitied him. "Tim-Tim!" she shouted as she threw her arms around him. "It's about time you showed up. I've been expecting you for two weeks."

"Good to see you, Margie. Don't worry. We'll soon get things all straightened out for you." As he said this, he eyed me up and down, no doubt deciding that I was what needed to be straightened out for Marge Meko.

"You sure will," she said, squeezing him extra tight to get the point across that this was an order. "That's Gary Gray, the *temp*." She threw a limp finger in my direction. I got the feeling that she wasn't so much introducing me, as she was pointing out the ugly mole she wanted removed.

Tim-Tim knit his brow and nodded at me in the same way the plumber nods when he identifies the hairball that is clogging up the pipes. I have to give Tim-Tim this much: he was not the least bit disingenuous in his attitude toward me. He made no attempt to shake my hand or mislead me into thinking it was his pleasure to meet me. In fact, he gave the distinct impression that he'd rather deal with a soggy hair ball.

Having identified the clog in Margie's works, Tim-Tim put aside all thought of me. "Well," he told Margie, "I'd better go set up so we can get this operation under way." He went into Steve's office, and with a wink back at Marge Meko, closed the door.

When Marge Meko turned to me, which she did as soon as the door closed, I knew what it felt like to stand in the glow of evil triumph in the devil's smile. "That's the auditor," she said, in the tone with which Robespierre might have pointed out the guy who trips the catch on the guillotine to Louis XVI. "He'll soon settle your hash."

Well, Louis XVI might have guessed that one day Robespierre would get a taste of his own medicine, but it did him no good in the meantime. Likewise, it did me no good to predict that one day Tim-Tim would choke on a spare rib and Marge Meko would be left to answer to an auditor for whom she had no pet name. The truth belched out of Marge Meko's mouth in her Satan's laugh: my hash was soon to be settled by a man named Tim-Tim. I wonder if King Louis's executioner had a pre-schooler's name.

Steve came in about 10 minutes later. Marge Meko's hellish smile refreshed itself. "Tim-Tim's in your office," she gushed.

"Right now?" asked Steve.

"Right now," Marge Meko affirmed. In my head, I heard her add, "Isn't it glorious?" but I don't think that part was real.

Steve was not in the habit of telling us where he was going, or when he'd be back, when he left the office, but Tim-Tim's sudden presence put Steve off his guard. "I've got to run out to my car. I'll be right back," he said.

"Don't take too long. Tim-Tim's waiting," Marge Meko told her boss.

Steve squinted hard at Marge Meko's boldness, but he held his tongue. That is, he held his tongue until he figured out that it would be all right to scold me for Marge Meko's uppity tone. "Gary, get this place straightened up, will you? Jesus, it looks like a pig sty."

I picked up a couple of papers from the counter and held them in my hand until he left. Then I put them back. It was Marge Meko's mess, and I was headed to the guillotine anyway.

Steve came back in a couple minutes. He didn't notice the papers back on the counter as he hurried to his own office. He was carrying something against the far side of his body. He hoped we wouldn't see what it was, but even more, he hoped we wouldn't see that he didn't want us to see it. So much for hope. It was one of those glossy, narrow gift boxes that hold a fifth of liquor. I probably wouldn't have seen it, except that it had obviously been

115

rolling around in Steve's trunk for a number of weeks, and he was trying to wipe off the dirt at the same time that he was trying to hide the box. I recognized it right away, because I've always wished that someday somebody would give me one. The liquor that I can afford to buy for myself never comes in a glossy box.

When Steve got to his office door, he reached for the handle, the way he had done a thousand times before. Instead of turning the handle, this time he stopped. He appeared to think a heavy thought for a moment; then he took his hand from the knob and knocked. His first knock was a little tentative, and it met with no reply. Steve frowned and knocked harder. A disinterested voice told him to come in. Steve put on a fake, fawning smile and opened the door. He tried to greet Tim-Tim as if they were old college buddies, but Tim-Tim must have cut him short. "No, I don't mind a bit," we heard Steve say. "Use my computer any time." As Steve shut the door on us, we heard him say, "Yeah, you're right. There are a lot of hot girls on that site."

The noise made by Steve's door closing was the sound of the end of my brief career in the accounting office of Appalachian Downslope College. The orders were making their way down the chain of command. From Marge Meko they'd gone to her corrupt kinsman. From Tim-Tim they went to the fiscally and ethically vulnerable, hence ass-kissing, Steve. Steve was in no position to refuse cutting loose a temp like me. Nor would he have much interest in refusing. If kicking me to the curb were the only price Steve need pay in order to relax and wallow in his irresponsible stewardship of the college's finances, he would consider himself to have gotten a freebie.

It was day's end before the orders worked their way down to me. Tim-Tim stepped out of Steve's office and gave me a long, blank stare. He nodded at Marge Meko the way a useful cousin in a crime family nods at the Boss to indicate that certain desired arrangements have been made. Marge Meko nodded back, assuring him that he had proved his loyalty once again.

Steve came out. He looked at Marge in the way the stooge of a useful cousin of a crime family, who has not yet earned the right to nod at the Boss, looks when he is executing certain desired arrangements. He didn't look at me, even as he spoke my name. "Gary, come into my office," is what I think he said, but what I heard was, "Gary. You and me, let's go for a little ride, eh?"

I walked into his office. I didn't need to look at Marge Meko to see the satisfaction on her face. When we sat down, Steve stared at some papers scattered across his desk. They were old invoices. "You know who that was who just left?" he asked.

I tried hard to look Steve in the eyes, but I couldn't find them. "Of course," I answered cheerfully. "That's Tim-Tim."

"Do you know who Tim-Tim is?"

"I gathered that he's the auditor."

Steve focused upon shuffling the invoices. "Do you know what an auditor does?"

Steve was floundering. I prodded him to cut to the chase. "As far as I can tell, he's like an accounting tooth fairy, except he takes away the good teeth and hides the rotten ones under the pillow."

Steve didn't note that my answer was sarcastic, only that it was incorrect. Therefore, he provided me with the correct answer. "The auditor checks to see that we have done our work correctly, so that we have not broken the law or needlessly wasted the college's money."

"That's a great idea," I said.

"Well, the auditor discovered that some mistakes have been made lately," Steve went on. "This stack of invoices I have here have all been double paid."

"I know," I said. "I brought them to you."

Steve didn't hear me, and he couldn't see my lips move because he wouldn't look at me. "Gary, this is a big waste of the

117

college's money and an embarrassment to the accounting department. We can't afford to have any more mistakes like this. I'm afraid we're going to have to let you go."

If he had just been honest and told me that Marge Meko was making him fire me, I would have left without a word. I understood that she had his balls in a vice. I knew I was going to be let go; it was simple arithmetic: two of Steve's balls in Marge Meko's iron grip equals one unemployed Gary Gray. He didn't have to try and smear my semi-professional, office worker reputation.

"Steve, Marge Meko paid those invoices, both times. Remember? I showed them to you and you asked me to try to recover the money; then you asked me not to recover the money. Are you now trying to say you think I double paid those?"

Steve sighed and swiveled away from me in his chair. "This isn't about trying to place blame, Gary. But I think the adult thing to do would be to own up to your mistakes. The adult thing would be to understand why we can't let this sort of thing go on," he tapped his hand on the pile of invoices, "and just go quietly without making any unnecessary fuss."

"Steve, you know those are Marge Meko's mistakes. Many of them are from before I even worked here. Go ahead , check the dates."

Steve gazed out the window as he replied. "Gary, you know I'm not one to go around pointing fingers. Your mistake?" He pointed at me. "Marge Meko's mistake?" He pointed through the wall toward Marge Meko's desk. "I doubt we'll ever really know for sure."

"Check the dates."

He took the stack from his desk and put them into a drawer. "The point is, we can't have this go on. Something's got to change. Look at it this way: Marge Meko's worked here for years, and the auditor never found a serious problem in all that time. You

118

work here a few months, and suddenly my desk is covered with critical errors."

"You want me to stop finding them?" That was a stupid question. "Of course you do. I learned my lesson the first time. I've overlooked a bunch of Marge Meko's errors since then."

Steve sighed again, more dramatically this time. There was nothing to see outside his window and he was getting tired of having to stare in that direction. "Gary, you're making this more difficult than it has to be. The fact that's clear is that you and Marge Meko don't work productively together, so I have to make a change. I'm sorry, Gary; that's just the way it is."

"So that's it then?"

"You can go home early today and I'll sign your time slip for five o'clock."

Who says temps don't get severance packages? It was 4:45 p.m. when I left Steve's office, so I got a nice deal worth 15 minutes of salary, and of course, by salary I mean hourly wages.

12.
Ask Not What Your Country Can Do for You; Help This Man Go Pee

I still have flashbacks to when I played pool against that guy who was in Nam. I'll get along fine for a while—seem to have it all put behind me—then Pow! It will hit me like a ton of bricks. It's worst at night. In the dark quiet of night it sneaks upon me, shattering the peace and spawning tumult within my head. War is a nasty thing.

Besides at night, the other time when I'm susceptible to my flashbacks is when I'm under a lot of stress. Even though I had just been fired from a lousy job, the prospect of being unemployed was daunting. Once the anxiety began to flow, I couldn't stop it. It swept me right back into that horrible memory, just like it was happening all over again.

It all happened before I met Gwen. I think that's why I can't talk to her about it. She could never really understand. You don't know anything about it until you've been there yourself. I was a free and easy single guy then. I had nothing better to do than hop from bar to bar, playing pool with all comers, and keeping an eye out for likely ladies.

I'd been out playing pool for quite a while one hot July night. It was getting late. The place was thinning out. Since there were not many folks interested in a game of billiards, I was boning up on my cue ball english all alone at the corner table. A few more shots and I probably would have packed it in for the night.

"Up for a little competition?" a gravelly voice asked from behind me.

"Only if you're willing to put your money where your mouth is," I said without looking away from the shot I was lining up. "I only play for beer." This statement was patently untrue. I was never good enough to play regularly for any type of wager. But it was late, and I was feeling good about the way practice was going, so I was willing to bet a beer on the chance that he might be worse than I am.

Without looking up, I very calmly and coolly took my shot, and missed badly.

"I'll take that action," the voice said.

"You're . . ." I turned toward where he sat in his wheel chair, legs missing, one sleeve of his tattered army jacket empty from the shoulder down. ". . .on."

He took no heed of my stammer. "Great," he said through his scraggly, graying beard as he wheeled himself with his one arm to the cue rack to pick out a stick. "You wanna rack 'em up, or you want me to?"

"I'll do it."

As I was racking the balls he examined a couple of cues. He held each one up to his face and peered down the length of it with the breathless intensity of a sniper sighting his target. I leaned out of his field of fire.

"You wanna break?" I asked.

"You racked, I get to choose. That's the way we did it back in the Delta." he said. "I'll let you go ahead and break."

I walked to the head of table and chalked my cue. I didn't want to beat up on the poor guy, but I wanted the game to be over quickly. I held nothing back on the break. Balls spread out into smaller clusters all over the table, but nothing went in.

"Nice break," he said as he craned to get a good look at the lay of the table. He brought his cue stick up over the lip, at which point I, and every other thing that wasn't on top of that table, faded from his sight. "LZ in sight. Time to jump off, boys," he said.

I was about to say, "Excuse me?" when I realized that he wasn't talking to me. He was talking to himself, or the billiard balls, or maybe even some friends who lived inside his head, but it had nothing to do with me. That was fine; I'm at my social best in a group situation anyway.

He held his cue out over the table with his one hand and rested the butt of the stick against his nose. Again, he peered down the cue with his sniper's gaze, lining up the shot with life-or-death carefulness. He was setting up to try to pick the three ball out of a cluster and nudge it into the side pocket. It was a shot I wouldn't even have attempted. "No. Take a shot that's reasonable, at least," I whispered to myself, now wanting the game to go especially quickly.

With as fluid a motion as I'd ever seen demonstrated at a billiard table, he rolled his shoulders, thrusting forward his nose, and the cue stick set against it. The cue ball rolled gently, caressing its object perfectly, coaxing the three ball out of its hiding place and depositing it cleanly into the side pocket. He made a clicking noise with his mouth, followed by, "Crow's nest emptied. Pillbox secured. Over."

I was as impressed by the shot as I was perplexed by the commentary. But since he didn't look to me for a response—he seemed to have forgotten my presence altogether—I kept my mouth shut and backed out of the way as he lay the cue across his lap and wheeled himself around the table.

The next shot he lined up was at a ball that lay at the opposite end of the table from the cue ball. Again, he rested the end of the cue stick against his nose as he zeroed in on the distant object. I don't know when I've ever seen someone so intently focused on something as he was on that seven ball down the table. In the stillness and quiet of his concentration, I imagined that he must be able to slow down his heartbeat like one of those Olympic biathletes. For a good five seconds before he shot, he was completely still. He didn't even blink.

An invisible shock wave sent me back a step as the quick flick of his head sent the cue ball speeding down the table. I couldn't have shot it any more smartly, with all the power of two good arms. There was a sharp tock as the cue ball sent the seven skidding into the corner pocket with authority. My adversary pulled his stick back from the table, looking admiringly at the business end of it. For a second I thought he was actually going to blow on it. Instead, he spoke to it. "One shot, one kill," he whispered to his pool cue.

The game went on like this, thankfully, not for very long. He wheeled himself around the table, sized up his shot, rested the cue on his face, became comatose for five seconds, then sent another round enemy soldier into a six-inch plastic grave. He began calling the balls "Charlie" and saying demeaning things to them as he, one by one, eliminated them in his cold, calculating way. This baffled me at first, but I eventually figured out what was going on. The whole Viet Nam thing went on before I was born, but I've seen the movies. After I made the connection, I just kept quiet, and found myself backing away from the table a half-step at a time.

If it hadn't been for all the post-traumatic stress in the room, it would have been quite a pleasure to watch him play. I'm not a billiards groupie or anything, but that one-armed man in that wheel chair was the best pool player I'd ever met. He knew the angles; he had perfect touch; he was a wizard with english. Then, just when you were ready to burst out with your spontaneous applause, he'd start telling the balls why God-less communists like themselves had to die.

I never took another shot against that man. The next active thing I did was buy him his beer. That was just after he had surgically removed the eight ball from a protective ring, formed by my untouched, striped balls, and deposited it securely into a corner pocket. He declared the sector secured over his invisible radio. Then he came back through the years, looked up at me for the first time since the game began, and let me know what brand of beer he preferred.

I was a little afraid that he would want to stick around and talk to me, while he drank his beer. No, that's not strictly true. Actually, I was afraid that he would want to stick around and make me wonder if he were talking to me as he made disjointed comments to billiard balls, or called in the co-ordinates for the air strike to the ether floating above his head. Once he got his beer, though, he seemed satisfied with the way the war was going in my sector. He wheeled himself away to another part of the bar as though he were quite through with me.

In order to seem like a good sport, I'd ordered myself a beer when I bought him his. Since half the balls were still on the table, I figured I'd knock them in while I finished the beer. I was a little rattled by what had just happened so I missed a lot of shots. Between drinking my beer, and shooting like crap, it took me half an hour to clear those seven balls.

I put up my cue stick. Turning around, I almost fell over the wheel chair. "Look, I'd love to play again, but it's past my bedtime," I explained.

"That's okay, buddy," he said. "I'm not interested in another game."

I must have given him a look like, "Well, why are you all rolled up on me, then?" I know that's what I was thinking.

"I need a favor."

"Oh shit!" I'm not sure whether I said it or merely thought it. I am sure that I thought it. I was thinking he was going to ask me something crazy, like to adjust the frequency on the plate in his head, because Charlie was intercepting his messages. I know it sounds cruel, but have you ever been in a situation like that? You would think the same damned kind of thoughts in those situations. You know damned well you would. You'd think, "I know he's a vet. He gave an awful lot for his country. That's great, and it deserves our respect and gratitude. But the man is crazy, and I've got a ton of things better to do than get mixed up in God-knows-what kind of favors for a nut case," because you know crazy people never ask simple favors. You know he's not going to ask you to pull something down from a high shelf for him. You know crazy people ask crazy favors, favors that are long and involved, and once you get into them, you can't get out, and you just need to be home in bed where it's safe.

Whether or not I said "Oh shit!" out loud, I am certain that I communicated it with my eyes. He must have been used to that look, because it didn't cause him a moment's hesitation. "Man, I been drinking beer for the past three hours straight. I really gotta go."

I looked at him through the blank eyes of growing fear.

"Dude, I gotta piss like a racehorse," he clarified.

A perfect blankness of the eyes may be, in fact, unattainable. Still, my eyes were racing toward that eternity as quickly as my accelerating fear could carry them.

"It's no big deal, man," he explained. "All I need you to do is hold me up in my chair. I can take care of the rest."

"Yeah?" I think I asked. I'm not sure why.

"Yeah. Believe it or not, I really can."

"Oh." I didn't know what else to say. I guess I was hoping that The Rapture, or something like it, would begin at that moment so I wouldn't have to say or do anything. I didn't even care if I were one of the chosen who ascended into Heaven or if I were one of those left behind—as long as my current companion was on the bus going the other way.

But The Rapture would not come, no matter how hard I

willed it. I resigned myself to the fact that I would have to get out of this by myself. "I don't know," I mumbled. "I'm not used to this sort of thing."

"Who the hell is? You think that guy in the corner is used to holding other guys up while they piss? You think it's no big deal to me that I need that kind of help? You think I like asking for it?"

My face grew warm as I began to feel like a selfish ass.

"Dude, it's no big deal," he continued. "You just stand there and hold me up for 30 seconds. You can keep your eyes closed the whole time."

Even feeling like an ass, I wasn't done hemming and hawing.

"Come on, man," he pleaded. "I can't hold it much longer. You gonna stand there and let me piss all over myself?"

This was a fine pickle. On the one hand, I couldn't see why my companion couldn't have asked that guy over in the corner for help. That guy looked like he was the type that talked under stall walls anyway. That was the kind of man for a job like this, not me, who didn't even like to acknowledge the presence of other humans in the bathroom. On the other hand, my companion had given both legs and an arm in the service of his country. All he was asking me to do was to hold him up for a few seconds, not dive on a live grenade. Even if he were just some guy in a wheelchair who needed a hand, that shouldn't be too much to do. But he was a veteran, probably a hero of some sort, and I'd be doing it not only for him, but for all veterans, for my country. Was holding a patriot upright while he peed too much for my country to ask of me?

In the end, the guilt got the best of me. I followed him into the men's room.

The room was empty, which eased my self-consciousness a good deal. He wheeled up to a urinal and, following his instructions, I took him by the armpits and lifted him. I didn't know if resting his weight on the stubs of his legs would hurt him, so I exerted myself trying to hold him aloft over his chair.

"Not so tight," he chided.

"Sorry, I didn't want to hurt your . . ." I couldn't refer to them as stubs, could I? ". . . legs," I whispered. Legs didn't seem like the right word either, but I had no idea what the official, disabled-friendly word might be.

He didn't seem to care about my gaff. "Don't worry," he said. "All that hurts right now is my bladder, and the place where you're trying to pull my arms off." That made me feel a little better, because he had said arms, when technically, he only had one complete arm. Either there wasn't an official, disabled-friendly word for the area that ends where limbs used to be, or he didn't know it either. So if he could say arms, I guess I could say legs.

I relaxed my grip on him and let him rest on his—you know—legs, while he went to work at his fly with his technically complete arm. I turned my head and looked to the side, but I could tell he was pretty adept at taking care of his trousers with one hand because I soon heard the telltale sounds of relief in progress. He wasn't kidding when he said he'd drunk a lot of beer that night. It seemed like I stood there holding him for 10 minutes.

I suppose it would have seemed like only five minutes, but you know how you get a terrible itch on the side of your nose at just the time when your hands are tied up and you can't scratch it? Well, my hands were firmly tucked into another man's armpits when my nose started to itch. Of course, there was nothing I could do but start twitching my face into the most unnatural contortions. Not only did that not work, but it somehow signaled to my back that it was a fine time for it to get an itch. Since my back wasn't getting scratched either, until the Exxon Valdez of bladders was done draining, I started rolling my shoulders and twisting my hips in a foolish hope that this would bring slight relief. Now, in the rational hindsight of relative comfort, I know that these efforts were forlorn; no one ever eased an itch by twitching it away. But when the itch hits you, you can't just stand there and do nothing. You've got to try something.

Just about the time when I reached the height of my facial and bodily twitching frenzy, the men's room door opened up and the guy who had been sitting in the corner walked in. He stopped short when he saw us. I believe he would have quickly come to terms with the sight of me holding up a legless man on his wheelchair so that he could pee. That's an unusual sight, but it makes some sort of logical sense once the picture gets processed. What really threw him was the fact that *I appeared to be dancing a rumba* while I was holding up a legless man on his wheelchair so he could pee. Not only that, I was twitching my face monstrously as I danced, very much like a man who was hearing the voodoo drums in his head. It did not soften the impression I surely was making that, when our eyes met, I stopped dead still, as if he had interrupted some sacred and diabolical rite. No one wants to be the intruder who brings the voodoo drums to a sudden stop.

It's difficult for me to imagine just how insane I must have appeared at that moment, but I'm sure that no matter how many arms and legs my companion might have lacked, I was the one who appeared least able to cope with the daily challenges of the wide world. That I was a frightening sight was proved by the quickness with which the newcomer scurried past us and threw himself into the stall. The audible securing of the latch on the inside of the stall door has never been so loud. There is no doubt in my mind that the man spent the whole time crouched on the floor in the far corner of the stall with his arms wrapped over his head. I am also quite sure that he stayed that way long after we had left, and never relieved himself one bit, but rather snuck out of the men's room, fled the establishment, and went screaming into the night.

Finally, I heard the flow from around front of my companion diminish to a trickle. A few elongated seconds more and he was ready to be lowered back into his seat. He sensed that I was ready to bolt. "Could you flush that for me?" he asked before I could pull free of him. "It's only good manners to flush when you're done," he told me, as if *I* had just finished something.

It's funny what revelations will come to you at odd moments. At that moment, I realized the useless, but seemingly profound, fact that I had never flushed for another man before. It seemed a shame to start then. I mean, I was on a 29-year streak of not getting embroiled in other men's business (so to speak), and this arrogant S.O.B. was glibly asking me to break that glorious trend as though it meant nothing.

He was right. It meant nothing. After what I had just been through, flushing was nothing. The man cowering on the floor of the stall might be able to keep out of other men's business for another night, but my streak was over. I pulled the urinal lever without further thought or ceremony. My proud past went down the drain.

My companion wheeled over to wash his hand. I stepped up to the sink next to his. My hands need to be washed after touching anything whatsoever in the men's room, which is problematic of itself because you generally have to touch things in order to wash your hands. But, you make the best you can of the situation. As we washed, our eyes met in the mirror, and suddenly I felt like he owed me a gratuity for what I had done for him. After all that, I should be able to ask him straight out about his wounds, without any fear of censure. "How'd it happen?" I asked, nodding generally toward him in the mirror. "Land mine? I heard those were nasty customers."

He looked puzzled for an instant. Then he chuckled, "Oh, you mean how'd I lose the pieces. Motorcycle wreck."

"In the middle of Viet Nam, you got messed up in a

129

motorcycle wreck?" I asked, sighing at the irony.

"No," he said. "I got in a motorcycle wreck in Louisiana. I've never been to Nam." He smiled as he wheeled himself to the door. "I've seen all the movies though."

That made two of us.

I know I told you that I still have flashbacks to when I played pool with the guy who *was* in Viet Nam. It's just easier for me to deal with if I think of it that way.

13.
Let's Fire Me Again, for Old Times' Sake

Gwen wasn't home when I got there, so I had a while to shake off my bad memories and figure out how to tell her I lost my job. I had been filling Gwen in about Marge Meko's antics all along, because they were entertaining, and because I wanted to prepare her for this inevitable day. Even having laid such groundwork, it wasn't going to be easy to break the news.

The more I thought about it, the more I drifted toward the conclusion that, not only would it be difficult to tell Gwen, it would sincerely hurt me to have to do so. Therefore, I made the only sensible decision and chose to put it off for a day or two. I would call the temp agency tomorrow. Maybe they would have something for me. Switching jobs would be far more palatable news than having no job. There was no sense in needlessly worrying Gwen when another job might just be a day away. I couldn't expect fate to be kind if I didn't give it a chance.

Just then, Gwen came through the door. "Hi honey," I said with a smile, proud of how contented and natural I was acting.

Even as I strode with lighthearted steps to greet her, her eyes narrowed. "What's wrong? What happened today?" she asked.

"What are talking about?"

She folded her arms. "Your greeting was off key, your smile is too symmetrical, and you're walking too much on the balls of your feet. Something's wrong."

Her keen sense of observation may be the death of me yet,

but not this night. The phone rang, and I answered it instead of answering her.

The lady on the phone was from Dynamic Temps. I had signed up with them at the same time I had signed up with Ready Temporary Service. Ready Temps had gotten me the job at Downslope College. I had heard nothing from Dynamic Temps, despite the active adjective in their name, since the day I signed up with them. I had almost forgotten that I was on their list of available workers.

This was quite a pleasant surprise. Not only had I never expected to hear from Dynamic Temps again, I certainly would never have expected them to contact me after five o'clock. But here it was going for six, and the one truly dynamic staffer the agency could boast was on the line offering me a position. My heart leapt when she told me she had a long-term position for me. My spirit soared when she told me I could start in the morning. Now I could just tell Gwen that I had exchanged my crummy old job, alongside crummy old Marge Meko, for a position with more potential for daily tranquility. That almost sounded like a responsible decision for me to have made. Gwen would appreciated that.

I plunged back to earth when the lady told me that the position was in the accounting department at Appalachian Downslope College. Apparently, the accounting department was so dissatisfied with their last temp that they not only got rid of him, they ditched his agency too. The lady took great amusement from that occurrence. She had great faith that I would be the one to prove to them, through the quality of my work, that Dynamic Temps was the right company to solve their temporary staffing issues.

I agreed with her. I had been ready to tell her that I had just left that job, until she made such a joke of how unhappy the employer had been with the work. Then I got annoyed that my performance had been besmirched and belittled into the joke of the day, making the rounds of the temporary service community. In response, there was nothing I could do but agree that I was the one to carry the banner of Dynamic Temps proudly into the accounting office at Appalachian Downslope College. I said that I was free and would be delighted to show up for work at eight in the morning.

I probably should have felt some anxiety about attempting such a stunt. If the assignment had been anywhere else, I would have. I would have been far too embarrassed to consider such a thing. But Steve and Marge Meko were people who owned no shame of their own. What right did they have to make me feel embarrassed about anything? Besides, I felt I still owed them a little bit of torment. One more chance to see Marge Meko shake with anger, and one more chance to see Steve fidget in discomfort, would be worth the worst of whatever humiliation people like that could make stick to me.

Steve and Marge Meko notwithstanding, I had Gwen left to deal with. By accepting this assignment, I could honestly tell Gwen that I had a job to go to in the morning. She already suspected I didn't, so I'd teach that smarty pants to go around reading me like a book.

The minute I hung up the phone, Gwen started in on me. "Who was that?" she asked.

"Lady from the temp agency."

"Why's she calling?" She looked at me sideways, like she does when she thinks she's getting a step ahead of me. "Did you lose your job?"

"Would I be going to work at the same place tomorrow if I'd lost my job?"

"What'd the agency lady want?"

"To know how things were going. They want to make sure their star worker is happy."

"Did you tell her you'd be happier if they found you a better job and paid you more?"

"I thought I'd try and be a bit more gracious than that."

"Gracious," she repeated. "That must be the reason I fell for you." She nodded and went about her business. I was not stupid enough to think that she was buying any of my bullshit. Gwen's too smart for that, but she's also too smart to need to trap me in my own bullshit every time, when sometimes I just need a little room to clean up my mess by myself. She's good at giving me a little slack sometimes, but don't worry, she'll swoop in and kick my ass if I really need it.

The next morning I spent 15 minutes searching the various drawers of our apartment for the time record form that Dynamic Temps had given me when I first signed up with them. I needed to present this triplicate form to my supervisor so that I could get paid for the hours I worked. Considering the circumstances, it probably wouldn't be all that useful to me, but I wanted it nonetheless.

"What are you looking for?" Gwen startled me out of my search.

"A pen," I lied.

"What do you need a pen for?"

"For work." This was a particularly bad lie, which Gwen picked right up on.

"They don't have pens in the accounting office?"

"Marge Meko chews on them all. I can't write with anything she's had in that mouth." That was a good save, but I had to continue my search covertly after Gwen handed me a pen. Fortunately, I soon remembered what I had done with the time slip. We had a hand-me-down desk in the corner of the bedroom with a short leg. I had folded over the time slip until it was a one inch by one inch square and used it to prop up the short leg. At the time, I'd figured that Dynamic Temps had forgotten all about me, so it seemed like a good recycling use of trash.

I put the wad of paper into my pocket and started out for my new assignment. I had my best tie on and an ironed shirt. Dynamic Temps could be proud to send such a young fellow as me to Appalachian Downslope College's accounting department as their representative.

In spite of the 15 minutes I had wasted, I was still early. I wanted to make a good impression. The door to the office was locked, so I waited in the hallway. Marge Meko was the first to appear. She snarled at me as she unlocked the door. "Forget something?" she barked.

"Pardon?"

"Did you forget something, yesterday?" she barked louder.

"Yesterday?" I gave her a puzzled look. "No ma'am. I don't believe so."

Marge Meko unlocked the door and I followed her in. I milled about in front of Steve's door while she unpacked herself. "What are you doing here, then?" she demanded.

"I'm waiting for Mr. Tallot." That was Steve's last name.

"Listen to you, acting all polite," she said. "Too bad it's too late for that. We've already got a new temp coming in today. Don't talk to them when they get here. I don't want them tainted."

I was trying to decide if I should innocently inform her that I was the new temp when Steve came in. By the way he looked back and forth between Marge Meko and me, I could tell he was trying to figure out if yesterday had all been a dream, or if today were some nightmare. "Why are you here?" he asked, having determined that yesterday was real.

"Dynamic Temps sent me over. I'm to start work for Mr. Tallot today."

Steve frowned. "Cut the crap, Gary. We're expecting the real temp any minute." He brushed by me and went into his office.

I followed him. "I assure you, I am the real temp."

He sat down hard in his chair. "We let you go yesterday, Gary. Why would we start over with you again today?"

"Because, it's a whole different situation." I pulled the time slip from my pocket and quickly unfolded it. I put the paper, with its many outlines of little squares, on his desk, pointing out the new logo on the top. "It's a totally new agency. I'm like a completely different temp this time. I'm practically a brand new Gary Gray. I swear, I won't notice any mistakes."

"They can't make us keep him, can they?" Marge Meko asked from the position she had staked out in Steve's doorway.

"Marge, can you please give us some privacy? I'll take care of this. I'll call the agency. Please close the door behind you."

Marge Meko made it clear, by the reluctance with which she exited, that she did not completely trust Steve's killer instinct. She would much rather have squashed me with her own chubby heel. Steve was weak, but for now, she'd allow him one last chance to finish the job.

Steve put the phone between his shoulder and ear. He needed both hands to smooth out the time sheet flat enough to be able to read the phone number on it. "Wait a minute," I said. "Before you call, there's one thing I want to say."

He rolled his eyes, but he put down the phone. "What?"

"You know that I'm not very inquisitive, when it comes to certain things that certain people around here may have done, or may be doing, with certain other people around here, that maybe they don't want to be widely known. I'd like you to consider this before you decide to bring a new person in here: what are the chances that anybody is going to be less inquisitive about such things than I have been? Do you really want to trade me for someone who is probably going to be a lot more interested in finding out who's doing what with whom in the janitor's closet? I've been here months, and I still don't know anything about such things." This was a lie. Why would I raise the subject if I didn't

136

know whose interests it affected? But I didn't expect Steve to discern the paradox. "Why don't I know? Because I don't really care. I'm here to earn some pay, that's all. But most people would find even the hint of such doings to be nice, juicy gossip. Who wants to be surrounded by rumor mongers?"

Steve knit his brow as he stared at the checkerboard-creased time slip in front of him. I knew he was thinking seriously about it, even before I caught him mumble, "That's a good point," to himself.

I was winning. I could visualize Steve signing his name to the bottom of the slip. I could see him sending me out to begin my assignment.

A breathless Marge Meko bumped the door open. "I just got off the phone with Tim-Tim. He's on his way over right now." She scowled at me. "He'll soon put an end to *this*."

"Marge, please!" Steve chided.

She gave him the stink eye and slammed the door shut.

"Gary, I appreciate all you've said, but I'm afraid the decision has been made." Steve told me. "We need to try someone new."

I didn't get up. Nor did I reply. I just sat there, staring from him to the ratty slip of paper on his desk. I knew it was over, but I wasn't quite ready to concede defeat at the hands of Marge Meko. There was nothing more to lose, so I just sat and stared.

"Say something," Steve begged.

I shrugged.

"You're not going to make this difficult, are you? Tim-Tim will be here before long, and I'd just as soon you were gone when he comes."

Finally, I had something to say. "Give me five minutes alone with Marge Meko out there. Then I'll go quietly."

"Why?"

"It's going to be an emotional goodbye, and I don't want

137

anyone to see me cry." Steve eyed me with suspicion. "Just don't come out for five minutes, and I'll be gone. Oh, and lock the door behind me. No matter what Marge says, don't let her in."

"What? Why?"

"Just do what I ask, and I'll be out of your hair for good."

"Promise?"

"Cross my heart."

"Okay. Just be gone before Tim-Tim gets here."

"Remember, lock the door, or you'll have Marge Meko in here blubbering all over you. She's very sentimental about me, you know." I was at the door before I remembered the time slip. "I'll need this," I said as I folded it back into its travel size. I had found nothing else that fit so well under the short desk leg. "Good luck," I said to Steve, and considering what he was left with, I think I meant it.

I began humming a happy tune as I closed the door behind me. Marge Meko's eyes were glued to me from the first. They grew larger and more desperate as I strode toward my erstwhile desk. As I sat down and booted up the computer, her mouth opened wide enough for me to fit my fist into it without scraping a tooth. "What are you doing?" she mouthed.

I spoke to her in a subdued tone, as if resigned to a fate that neither of us wanted. "Steve called the temp service. I have to stay here. There's no other way."

In increasingly bright shades, Marge Meko turned purple. "No! That's a lie!" But even this steadfast declaration didn't quite seem sure of itself. As quickly as she could extract herself from her chair, she was at Steve's door. She didn't bother to knock, but went straight for the handle. The door wouldn't budge. "Open this door, Steve Tallot! I know you're in there!" she demanded.

Not a peep could be heard from beyond the door.

I stood beside Marge Meko's desk looking over the papers spread out there. "Steve asked me to double check your work," I told her as she listened for noise of life from within Steve's office. "He said you've been slipping lately."

"Steve, I need to talk to you, right now!" She threw her shoulder against the door, and I really thought it might give.

"You mind if I start with these?" I flipped the corners of some of her papers.

My five minutes weren't up yet, but I feared that Steve might break and open the door. It was time to let them begin the first day of their new lives together. "Marge Meko, you don't look well at all. Maybe you should sit down and try to relax for a while. I'm going to get you some water." I went to the hall door and gave the office one final look, never intending to come back. Marge Meko's head looked ready to explode. It would be something to see, but probably messy. I walked out.

Tim-Tim was just coming down the hall. He passed me, then stopped and looked back. "Aren't you the temp that Steve fired yesterday?"

I raised an eyebrow at him. "Fired? You must be thinking of Marge Meko. Steve fired her and gave me her job." The color ran out of Tim-Tim's face. He sprinted toward the accounting office. As much as I would like to have seen both Marge Meko and Tim-Tim pounding on Steve's door, I decided to keep going.

14.
Who Among You, Oh Drunken Unemployed, Will Take Elvis His Bourbon?

Well, now I was going to have to admit to Gwen that I had indeed lost my job. It would be extra awkward after I had played so indignant at the suggestion the night before. It would be several hours before I would have to tackle that, however, and an age-old instinct told me how to best spend that time.

Why is it that when a man loses a steady income, the first thing he must do is rush out and spend money he does not have on something he does not need? Of course, I am speaking of liquor. There seems to be some kind of spiritual connection between fresh unemployment and a couple of stiff belts. Is it that men are so intrinsically boring that we can think of no other way to fill the time with which we now find our hands full? Do we spend our last few dollars because we need to be drunk and penniless in the gutter of life before we can tell which direction is up? If I am any example of man, the answer is not either of these. The answer is that we feel the need to both fortify and benumb ourselves before the time comes to face up to our women.

If man didn't have woman to confess his failures to, I expect he could lose job after job with impunity. The time on his hands would be light and tickling as a feather. He could spend that first unemployed afternoon climbing trees and playing in creek beds. He could eat wild berries and dirt for dinner, and be happy. He could have a taste of his childhood and really enjoy it, before the world goaded him into seeking to become productive again. He could quit worrying about having to be a man, if only for a little while.

But when there is a woman to answer to, a man must endeavor to come up with a plan, or at the very least, excuses. He sits with his bottle and drinks and thinks until he comes up with some hare-brained speech that holds no hope of placating his woman. Luckily, the bottle lovingly hides the no hope part and thus prevents him from just running away to the circus. In the end, he goes home to face her, because thanks to liquor, he doesn't know any better.

Even the best of women cause this reaction. It need not be intended. Perhaps it is especially the best of women who cause it. The better the woman, the more bitter the man's humiliation at having failed her. Besides, if a man must be goaded back into being productive, it is probably better that he has no chance to taste the sweets of childhood first. It's better that he feels guilty and gets drunk, and is driven to seek out new work as soon as he is sober again, than that he figures out what he's missing.

The upshot of all this rationalization was that I made a stop at the liquor store on the way home. Gwen must be having a good effect upon me, because in earlier days I would have embraced the self-destructiveness of the situation and splurged on a top-shelf whiskey. This time I had the limited good sense to give a passing thought to the need to buy groceries at week's end. As a result, I still upheld my commitment to down-trodden, self-pitying man syndrome, but I did so with a much more cost-effective, lower-shelf selection.

At home, I soothed my flagging spirit by turning on Jerry Springer. It was comforting to see that there were people who were, at once, more pitiful and more self-destructive than I. And people say that Jerry's guests add nothing to our society. I made a solitary toast to them with my first shot.

It was still quite early in the day, so I determined myself to take my liquor slowly. With each sip I felt myself more sensitive. I needed to share my feelings. Moreover, I needed to share my cheap fifth of whiskey. Alone, I was in danger of finishing the whole thing myself, which was a more self-destructive display than I thought myself equal to. I called my friend Len. Len, if you don't recall, is the guy who got all bent out of shape because I didn't say hello to him in the men's room. Len was mostly over that slight by now. He got completely over it when I told him I was handing out shots. As a philosophy student, he finds spirituous drink to be a very helpful, but rarely affordable, commodity.

"What's the occasion?" Len asked as he settled into the recliner with glass of whiskey.

"Since when did a philosopher ever need an occasion to drink whiskey?" I answered.

"Never. But I'm talking about *you* drinking whiskey in the middle of the day, instead of being at work." Even as he said it, the engine of logical argument revved up enough to light the bulb inside his head. "Oh," he said. "That's a rotten break. What happened?"

"I wasn't corrupt or stupid enough for them. So I got to be the odd man out."

Len took a sip and produced the following philosophical analysis. "Bummer."

"I can't wait to tell Gwen."

Len sighed. "Yup. The worst part of having a woman is having to tell her when you fuck up."

"Especially when your fuck up was trying to do your best."

"Yeah, it sucks. Women don't believe in over-achieving fuck ups. They always think you fucked up cause you're lazy and you don't care."

In all Len's years of philosophizing, this was about the brightest pearl he had come up with. "I'll drink to that," I told him.

As we were toasting Len's wisdom, the three-way bulb in his head kicked itself up to a higher wattage. "Dude!" he blurted. "Weren't you just a temp anyway?"

"Yeah. So?"

"So? I was over here trying to help you wipe away your tears and drown your sorrows cause I was thinking you lost some sweet job, with benefits and paid vacation and everything. Dude, it was a temp job! Who the fuck cares? You were filling space till some chick came back from having a kid or something. That's why they call it a temporary position; it's not supposed to last forever."

"But it was money coming in," I protested. "Money we need."

"Judging from this rot-gut we're drinking, it wasn't much. Besides, there's got to be hundreds of other chicks getting ready to spit out kids. Go keep one of their seats warm for a while. Better yet, take the rest of the summer off. Enjoy life before you're too old."

"Yeah, it's about time for my annual trip to Graceland to leave a bottle of bourbon on Elvis's grave anyway." I don't know where that comment could have come from except for the whiskey. I was not of the Elvis generation; in fact, he was dead before I was born. I was not an Elvis fan. I actually knew very little about him that wasn't parody or exaggerated imitation. I'm not even sure how I knew that Graceland was his home. Not only had I never gone there, with or without the gift of bourbon, but I had never even thought of going there. Even as I spat out these words of ersatz sarcasm, I would not have dreamt of making such a trip.

Len's eyes lit up. "Dude? Really? No way? I never knew you did that. That's so cool! Elvis rocks! I mean, he died on the toilet. How cool is that? That's the way I want to go, I mean, all purged of earthly soils like that, all relaxed, cleaned out, and ready

143

to meet God."

"Elvis died on the toilet?" It was news to me.

"Of course he did. How else would The King go, but on the throne? Wouldn't you want to go out like that?"

"I'd prefer to wash my hands first."

"Cool, man. When are you going?"

I absolutely thought that he was talking about the toilet now, and buzzed though I was, I wasn't quite ready to talk about schedules for such things. "I don't know."

"Can I come with you?"

Considering how much Len seemed to like to chit chat in the men's room, I shouldn't have been surprised. Chit chat was one thing; I was growing worried that he was coming up to the idea of a potty suicide pact or something. "No," I said sternly. "I think it's something I ought to do by myself."

"Aw man! Come on! It would be such a blast. I've never been to Memphis before."

"Memphis?"

"Yeah, Memphis."

"What about it?"

"Dude, focus! Watch my lips: When are you going on your annual trip to Graceland?"

I guess, somewhere in the back of my mind, I knew that Graceland was in Memphis, but never having been there, I wasn't sure. I also recollected that my unrecognized bit of sarcasm about leaving an annual gift on Elvis's grave was the root of this whole arcane conversation. Mostly, I was relieved that Len wanted to go to Graceland with me and not to the bathroom. These convergent revelations, but mostly the liquor, made me laugh. I laughed for a good while, till I was sick of it and Len was pissed at me. Then I stopped. I got very calm and said the most reasonable thing I could imagine. "I'm not. I've never been to Graceland in my life."

"Don't be an ass," Len told me. "If you really don't want

me to go with you, just say so."

"Len, if I were going to Graceland, you would be the first person I would invite along. But I'm not. I don't even know if Elvis likes bourbon. I made the whole thing up. I was trying to be sarcastic."

"Well, you're not very good at it, which sucks, because taking a bottle of bourbon to Elvis would be a blast."

"Probably would."

"Shit, man!" Len shook his head in disgust. Then he said something completely different. "Shit, man!" It was different because his head popped up as he said it and there was a gleam in his eye. "Shit, man!" he repeated, almost bursting into song, "We should do it. We should go."

It didn't take much for Len and the bottle to convince me that this trip was a great idea. By the time Gwen came home, our plans were as nearly complete as the bottle was empty. Gwen was a little surprised to find both Len and the empty bottle in our living room, but she rolls with the punches pretty well, and she is willing to let boys be boys once in a while, so long as they are no threat to themselves or others.

Meanwhile, Len was pretty excited about the plans we'd made, and he saw no need to let me gently bring Gwen up to date, or to let her put two and two together. "Guess what," he said to her. "We're going to Graceland."

"We are?" she humored him.

"No, not we. *We*." He slung his arm back and forth between himself and me. "Me and Gary are driving down to Graceland."

"The *Elvis* Graceland? When?"

"Thursday." It was now Tuesday afternoon. "We'll come back on Sunday."

"Oh. Gary doesn't have to go to work on Thursday or Friday?" She asked my travel agent this question, but she looked squarely at me.

"Nope. He got his ass fired. He's free as a bird."

"I see. And Gary thinks the best way to recover his precarious financial situation is to joy ride to Memphis, rather than looking for another job?"

"Yup. That's what I got from him."

"Well. I have to say, that's a rather ingenious plan. It's amazing what two boys and a bottle of whiskey can come up with all on their own."

"Yeah, I know." Len was no better at catching Gwen's sarcasm than he was at catching mine. He'll make a great philosopher some day. "You haven't heard the best part though. We're going to stop in Kentucky on the way and pick up a bottle of top-notch bourbon, cause everybody knows, if you want real bourbon, you've got to get it in Kentucky. Then we're going to leave the bourbon on Elvis's grave. Isn't that awesome?"

Gwen nodded. "It's good to know that we've got money to buy dead Elvis nice things. I'm sure the groundskeeper will appreciate your thoughtfulness."

I probably should have piped up and spoken for myself at some point, but it was easier to let Len hold forth for me. I was a little taken aback by the way he just blurted out that I'd lost my job, but then, that did save me a lot of hemming and hawing, trying to get the words out myself. I had dreaded having to tell Gwen that I'd lost my job, and now I didn't have to. Also, I would have been the most timid sheep in the world trying to explain to her why Len and I needed to throw expensive bourbon at the Graceland support staff. Len, with all his enthusiasm, made it seem like a much more worthwhile endeavor, to me at least.

I didn't say a word until Gwen had maneuvered Len out the door. Afterward, I didn't say much either. Gwen was pissed off: not because I had lost my job, not because I had spent a few bucks drowning my misfortune in cheap whiskey, not even because of the cockamamie scheme to drive to Memphis. She should have been pissed off at the latter, but she didn't think it would outlive the effects of the whiskey. Gwen was pissed off because the night before, when she had asked me if I had lost my job, I had strongly insinuated that I had not, and that for her to ask such a question demonstrated a lack of faith. This, in her morally organized world, was equal to a bald-faced lie. Furthermore, she was sure that I had gotten dressed and gone out this morning in an effort to perpetuate that lie, knowing damned well that I had no job to go to.

Gwen was pissed, so she didn't have much to say to me. I knew she had a right to be pissed, so I kept quiet. It was best to let her storm of silence pass.

In the morning things were nearly back to normal. Gwen was still a little upset, but she was trying her best to put it behind her. I'd screwed up. I hadn't been as forthcoming as a man ought to be with the woman he hopes will someday consent to marry him. That was unfortunate, but it was done, and it could not be undone. Gwen has never been one to waste time trying to scrub out an indelible stain. She'll find a way to put the stain out of sight and get on with her life. Of course, she has been known to throw an item out and start anew when it has collected too many stains to turn out of sight. So I tried not to broaden the ugly spot on my character by attempting to explain it away.

The other thing that wasn't quite normal in the morning was that I had nowhere to go. In a day or two, Gwen would be curious as to what constructive things I planned to do with my free time, but on this morning, she would not ask. She would go about her own business and allow me to figure out a plan before she would demand the details of it. I appreciated that, because I didn't know how I would spend my unpaid day. It was nice not to have to say that aloud.

Things might have gotten right back to normal after that

day, except that I knew exactly how I was going to spend the next four. I fully intended to travel to Memphis with Len. Gwen, on the other hand, had put all such nonsense right out of her mind. I brought it right back into her mind when she found me packing a bag that night.

I had pushed her forbearance over the edge. This was too much for her, and she let me have it. I tried to uphold my pride by giving it back, but deep down, I knew I was the unreasonable one. It's hard to argue with someone who's right. It's like trying to cling to a bit of wreckage after the ship's gone down. It takes a lot out of you, and it doesn't get you any closer to solid ground.

I kept treading water in my own unreasonableness till Thursday morning when Len came to pick me up. I tried to say goodbye to Gwen normally, as if a good night's rest had put everything to rights. The fatal flaw in my reasoning was that nobody in our house had gotten a good night's rest. If anything at all had been put to rights, Gwen didn't mention it. She didn't say a word. I felt a twang at her silence, but I was determined to stick to my guns.

I felt better when I got into Len's car. I gathered that he was excited about our coming adventure by the way he repeatedly yelled, "Road trip, baby!" in my ear. Before we could navigate through the parking lot of our complex he reiterated how much fun we were going to have at least 16 times. Only as we stopped at the exit of the lot did he utter a phrase that did not make him do a little rumba in his seat. "Dude, we're gonna need some gas right away."

"No problem," I reassured him. "I'll get the first fill up. You get the next."

He sat perfectly still as he made his next statement. "I was hoping you could take care of most of the gas on this one. I'm a little short of funds just now."

"I thought we were gonna split the gas down the middle."

"Sorry dude, I'm just a little tapped out right now. I was

hoping you could spot me a little credit on that and the hotel bill, till I get back on my feet again."

"The hotel too?"

"Yeah. I'll make it up to you. No big deal, right?" Traffic had cleared and he was about to pull out onto our wonderful road trip, fully funded by me.

"Len, wait."

"Wait what? I'm all set to go." He made a face like it pained him to miss this golden opportunity to pull out into traffic.

"Wait. I can't be paying for this whole trip. I'm unemployed." Then it snuck out. "God knows, I shouldn't be going at all."

"Dude, it's all good. I'll get you back one of these days."

"I can't afford it right now."

"Dude! Will you relax!" Len exploded, as if he were the reasonable one. Then I understood how Gwen had been feeling for the past two days. "Let's just go have a good time. The money will sort itself out."

"I don't know what bank you use, but mine doesn't offer the sort-itself-out money market account. My money doesn't do anything by itself but disappear, and somebody, probably me, should start keeping a closer eye on it. And by the way, I fucking hate it when you call me dude."

If this outburst gave Len pause, he didn't use the pause to think about the outburst. "Dude, I've been calling you dude since sixth grade."

"And I've been fucking hating it since sixth grade."

"Dude! Man! You've got issues!"

"Thanks for bringing that up, because until this moment, I didn't realize how many issues I have." It was true. I'd needed to do a comprehensive inventory of my issues. I suppose it didn't really matter if I counted up all the many minor issues clogging up the back of my mind; I needed to identify the big ones. The one

149

standing right out front was that I had been lucky enough to find what I'd always wanted most, and I was starting to run away from it because I'd begun to doubt that I deserved it.

I did have just about enough money in the bank to support Len and myself through a four-day weekend. Even in lean times, I had been saving up a little bit every month. All the while I told myself that I was saving it because it was the responsible thing to do, and that it was good to have a little put aside, just in case times got even leaner. If that were true, I probably could have convinced myself to blow it on this trip. But it wasn't true.

I'd saved a tiny fraction out of every paycheck because there was a very specific object that I was building up the nerve, and the combination of cash and credit, to buy. I had saved because I wanted to believe that I could keep what I had been lucky enough to find, always and forever. I had saved because, if I believed that one day I could at least present a token of my deservingness, it might hold off the fear that I was just another irresponsible fraud. I had saved because I wanted Gwen to know that I appreciated all that she deserved, even if I were never able to give her the half of it.

I had not saved in order that Elvis's ghost, or his groundskeeper, whichever got it first, could get shit-faced on top-notch Kentucky bourbon. I had not saved because dying on the toilet, even if it were true, earned the dead some sort of martyrdom worthy of a four-day pilgrimage. I had not saved so that I could be referred to as Dude for four days straight by somebody who should have learned my name in elementary school. And I certainly had not saved so that Len could travel the earth without need of gas money.

"Can we get going already?" Len prodded.

"No." I grabbed my bag and got out of the car. "You can go. I'm staying home where I belong."

"What the hell, man? I can't go without you. I got no gas.

150

Jesus, Gary!"

"Dude!" I yelled. "That sucks!" I slammed the door closed and walked back to my place.

I didn't say a word to Gwen. I just marched right up, took her in my arms and kissed her the best way I know how.

"I thought you were on your way to taking Elvis his bourbon," she said, once I'd let her mouth free.

"Elvis can get his own damned hooch," I said. Then I kissed her again.

15.

You Too Can be a College President

I figure I'll eventually end up as the president of Appalachian Downslope College. I'll be the first one ever to achieve that title as a temporary worker. I'll have to get my secretary to sign off on my time sheet every week, and I'll be raking in about $13 an hour, but otherwise, it'll be pretty prestigious. Appalachian Downslope College just can't seem to get enough of my sweet love.

Ready Temps was the culprit this time. They didn't mind at all that I had just been discharged from the accounting office of the very same institution. That just made me another warm body with time on his hands. With such impeccable credentials, it was a shame to leave me floating around in their inactive pool.

There was a vacancy in the college president's office and, by God, Ready Temps was going to fill it if they had to dredge every swamp in the county to find a worthy creature. Fortunately, I had recently come available, so maybe they could snatch me back up and save themselves the rental on the excavating equipment.

I was willing enough to work, but a little wary of renewing my relationship with Downslope College. My wariness, I was assured by the bubbly, teen-aged-sounding voice of the account executive from Ready Temps, was unfounded, as this new position required no accounting skills. Little did she know that accounting skills were not appropriate for my last assignment either. I did not mention this to her, however, as I feared it would lead her to conclude that my discharge had resulted from a lack of some other skill.

I was still a little daunted, even after I accepted the assignment, but when I had time to consider it in more depth, my worries began to fade. Yes, I had a checkered history with Downslope College, but that was pretty well contained within the accounting department. Even though I'd not had an accounting background, in that particular department I still turned out to be the man who knew too much. How likely was that to happen again?

Thankfully, I knew nothing of a college president's duties. I had no idea what it might take to steer the collegiate ship through the waters of higher learning. Hence, my ignorance would be my bliss. The boss man could make any kind of presidenting errors he wished, and certainly I would be none the wiser. I would go right along and say, "Yes, sir," bow my head in deference, file the mistake away safely in a cabinet, go home feeling satisfied with a good day's work, and sleep soundly through the night. I would become the model employee, always sporting a clueless grin, without the faintest trace of doubt at the corners of my eyes. I would be patted on the back and have my hair mussed, and I would be invited to the annual picnic, for no better reason than that I was a threat to no one.

Best of all, I would never have to battle the nagging temptation to squint and ask, "Are you sure you want to do that?" I would keep my opinions to myself, because—praise be to God!—I would have no opinions of my own. The president could drive the collegiate ship into the rocks, and I would gladly drag myself to the beach because, for all I would know, the rocks might be the perfect place for the ship, and the beach the perfect place for me and the bloated bodies of the less fortunate.

After a while of these musings, my mind slipped into a dreamlike stupor of glee. My potential within the loftiest circles of Downslope College was limitless, so long as I resolved myself not to learn. I would make a long career of being an edu-temp. I would move up the ranks by marshaling the combined power of natural attrition, being in the right place at the right time, and incessant smiling. I would become such a steady fixture of the campus that eventually somebody would offer me health care. Then, I'd be set for life.

I had just achieved this sublime state when Gwen came home. I could not wait to tell her the news. She would be so happy for me. How could she be anything less? Our problems were at an end. "Honey, I got a new job!" I blurted as she came through the door.

Her eyes brightened. "Really? Where?"

"The president's office." I gushed, as if that were all anyone need hear to know exactly where I would be, and that it was the best job ever.

"The president of what?"

"The college, of course."

Her bright eyes darkened. "Downslope College?"

"The only college in town!"

She sighed like a mother. "Hon, you just got fired from there."

"This is different. This is the president's office. I'll do great there."

"How do you figure?"

"Listen," I said as I began to unfold my master plan. "Put me in the accounting office over there, and I'm automatically a relative genius. People in colleges don't like geniuses. But in the president's office, I'll be stupid."

"How are you going to be stupid?"

"Ignorant, actually. Look, I don't know the first thing that's supposed to go on in the president's office, and as long as I keep it that way, they're sure to love me."

She rubbed her forehead a little bit. "Gary, have you ever

thought about when it would be a good time to start looking for a permanent job?"

"I am looking for a permanent job. All the time. Every time I take a new assignment, there's the chance it could turn into a permanent job."

"A chance. Why not just get a permanent job to start with?"

"Because, studies have shown that more and more employers are testing out new hires as temps first, before making them permanent."

"Studies? Which studies?"

"I don't know their names. But I read all about them on the Internet at my last job, in between my discoveries of Marge Meko's accounting errors."

She stopped rubbing her head, then thought better of it and started rubbing again. "That's just my point. Maybe if you got a *real* job, where you had *real* work to do, you could show them how smart you are and be able to work your way up to a better position."

"Oh, don't worry. I plan to work my way up in this next job."

"What kind of work will you be doing?"

"I don't know."

"Will it be challenging at least?"

I thought about everything I knew about Appalachian Downslope College. "Almost certainly not," I answered.

"So there will be no way for you to prove to them that you're not just another stupid dolt."

"Stupid dolt like a fox." I tapped my forefinger against my temple. "Like a fox."

That was enough for Gwen. She had to walk away and decompress for a while. I guess I understood her concerns, but she just didn't understand my master plan. One day she'd see. When I was the senior temp in all of Appalachian Downslope College, she'd see.

Over the weekend, Gwen came to terms with my new assignment and my enthusiastic embrace of all its opportunity. I think she figured it couldn't be any worse than my last assignment. The money was the same, and as far as she was concerned, it would be just like when I worked in the accounting office, except that she wouldn't have to hear me rant about Marge Meko. It wasn't the job she would have chosen for me, but then my judgment skills must be improving, as evidenced by the fact that I had not blown my savings going to see Elvis. She made the wise decision to let me evolve into a responsible adult at my own pace, so long as I was showing some progress.

By Monday morning, when she kissed me and wished me good luck, there was no sign that her heart wasn't in it. She's good at making the best of things, which is an absolute necessity for anyone who is tangled up with me. As the one thing in my life that I hope is not temporary, Gwen's support means a lot. It's especially important when my optimistic plans for the future are built on quicksand.

The lady on the phone had told me to report to someone named Ray. The first person I came across, upon entering the president's suite, had his back toward me. His hair was cut square in the back but it covered his ears. He was wearing black slacks and a dress shirt. He was also wearing white shoes, which I thought a little odd, but maybe that's what the president's men do. "Excuse me," I said. "I'm looking for Ray."

The man turned around. "I'm Ray," he said in a voice higher pitched than I'd expected. The voice was nothing, though, compared to his pink lipstick and his costume earrings.

I put out my hand. "I'm Gary Gray. The temp agency sent me." Ray's handshake was limp and clammy.

"Good. Follow me," Ray instructed. I had been almost

convinced that Ray was a woman, but his lumbering walk forestalled that conclusion.

Ray led me past three women typing away on their keyboards to a desk in the back corner of the suite. "There. This is your workstation," he said. "Make yourself comfortable."

"Thanks," I said. I tried to scrutinize Ray's features as well as I could, without gawking. I found myself again leaning toward the conclusion that Ray was a woman.

"It'll be nice to have another man around the office," Ray said, in what I could only regard as a flagrant attempt to try to confuse me more.

I wanted to ask, "Another man besides who?" but I thought I should begin at the beginning. "I have a stupid question for you," I said.

"Yes? What is it?"

"Are you—I feel embarrassed even having to ask this—are you the college president?"

Ray put an open hand on his chest and blushed. "Oh no. What a wild idea! No, I'm just President Burton's executive assistant." He took his hand from his chest and put his fingertips on my shoulder as he chuckled. "We better put you to work before you make me queen."

I nodded. I didn't want to get involved in that transformation.

He took a pile of letters from the desk tray and laid them down before me. "Here's my mail. The first thing I'd like you to do is take that letter opener there and open all these envelopes. When you're done, put the stack in the rack beside my office door. You see that door before the corner office? That's President Burton's office. The next one, the corner office, is mine. That's where you put the mail when you're done opening it. Got it?"

"Got it," I assured him.

"Good," he said. That was all. He went away.

Right away I noticed that the name on the envelopes was Billie Rae Horn. That fairly well convinced me that Ray, a.k.a. Rae, was a woman. But watching her walk away like a ranch hand, I would still bet that she peed standing up.

Turning to the work at hand, I began opening Billie Rae's envelops with zeal. This was just the sort of mindless work that would make me a star in the academic clerical world. I was just getting into my pick, rip, stack rhythm when I was stopped short by an envelope addressed to Peter Burton, President. Now, this wasn't the type of crisis I was ready to overcome on my way to the top. Rae had clearly instructed me to open the stack of envelopes, but she had intimated that all the envelopes were addressed to her. Surely, she did not intend that I open her boss's mail and put it into her rack.

Well, I would do the sensible thing and put that letter aside until I had finished the stack. I had another good 30 seconds worth of envelopes to open. There was no sense worrying my pretty little head over the stray before that. So, I moved the letter to the bottom of the pile and prepared to attack the next one. I'll be damned if that one wasn't addressed to Peter Burton too. I flipped through all that were left. They were all for him. So much for my 30-second grace period.

It was the age-old conflict between following orders and displaying a little common sense. The problem with this dilemma is that there's no right answer. It all depends on whether your supervisor wants you to be a blind follower or a leader of the blind. I couldn't tell that about Rae yet—hell, I wasn't even sure which restroom she used. That meant I would have to break down and do the unthinkable.

I had not planned on having to ask for clarification of anything within the first five minutes of work, but I had also forgotten to give Rae my time sheet, so I could use that as an ice breaker. The corner office door was open. Rae was sitting at her

158

desk staring at her computer. Her hands were primed on the keyboard, as if she were ready to fly into productivity at any moment, but that moment wouldn't come. I knocked on the door frame.

She looked up. Her fingers tensed. "Sorry to interrupt," I said, "but I forgot to give you my time sheet." Her fingers flew into action as I spoke. I could swear she was typing my words.

"Put it in the rack with the mail," she said as she typed.

"Sure thing." I said. She typed a short burst. I pretended to turn away and then catch myself. "Oh, one more thing," I dictated to her awaiting fingers. "There were letters for President Burton in the pile of mail you gave me. What should I do with them?"

Her face turned sour. "You need to open all the envelopes and put them in my rack, just exactly as I instructed you to do." Her tone was scolding and I'm sure she typed it out in all caps. "When you're done with that, Tina has work for you to do."

I assumed Tina must be one of the three women working in the outer office. "Which one is Tina?"

She typed another burst, then stared at her monitor as if to see in black and white my ridiculous question. "She's the older one."

"Okay, great," I replied. As I turned away I heard the spurt of two words being typed.

Well, at least I would know to whom I should report next, without having to go back and interrupt Rae again. I just had to find the oldest one of the women. I got a good look at all three as I returned to my work area. Each one of them was exactly between 28 and 45—not one day older, nor one day younger.

After I had finished opening Rae's presidential mail, I approached the nearest of the women. She had red hair. "Which of you ladies is Tina?" I asked. She nodded in the general direction of the woman with blonde hair. The problem was that this was also in the general direction of the woman with the brown hair.

159

I went next to the blonde. "Tina?" I asked.

"Oh no, Hon," she said with a subtle southern accent. "I'm Sherrie. That's Tina." She pointed to the brown-haired lady.

"Sorry," I said.

"Don't worry about it, Sugar. You'll get to know us all well enough pretty soon."

"Tina?" I asked the brunette.

"Third time's the charm," she said with an expression that was either a smile or a mild angina attack.

"Yeah. Rae said you had some work for me."

"Sure do. But I should warn you, the new guy always gets the worst of it here. You get to do math."

"That's okay," I said. "I used to work in an accounting office."

"Oh." She got a look in her eye like I could be useful to them. "You're an accountant?"

"Not even close." I hated to disappoint her, but I had to clear my name.

Tina took me back to my work area and instructed me to open an electronic spreadsheet on my computer. It was a record of various professors and scores they had received on their student evaluations. After several columns of scores, the far right column was labeled AVERAGE. This column was blank. Tina informed me that I was to use a hand-held calculator to figure the average of each row of scores and type that number into the far right column. As she explained, I nodded along, as if that were a perfectly reasonable way to do it.

"Do you know how to figure out an average?" she asked.

"Yes. I'm pretty sure I do."

"All right then. You just let me know if you have any problems with it. I'll be right over at my desk there. Now don't try to go too fast. You might want to take a little break every hour or so. All that calculating gets to you after a while."

"All right," I said, appearing grateful for the advice. When she walked away, I typed in the formula for calculating the average in the top row of the far right column. I dragged it down to the bottom. It hadn't been an hour, but I figured it was time for a break, considering that there was nothing left for me to do on this task. I went to the Internet and checked out my favorite sports sites. Every so often I tapped randomly with my fingers on the buttons of the turned off calculator. As long as they kept me in the back of the suite, where nobody could see my monitor, this might turn out to be an okay job.

After an hour, Tina approached. I closed the Internet browser and acted like I was concentrating hard on the spreadsheet. "Everything okay back here?" Tina asked. "I noticed you haven't been using the calculator too much lately."

Her words made me realize two things. First, I had gotten so involved in sports that I'd neglected to keep up my random tapping at the calculator. Second, this Tina lady was a little bit on the nosey side. Before she could come around behind me, I opened up the calculator on my desktop. "No, I've been using the calculator on the computer. I find it easier to use," I said.

Her eyes grew wide as she spied the calculator window on my screen. "Your computer has a calculator right on it?" she asked. "If I'd known this was the *good* computer, *I* would have taken it. I need that on *my* computer."

Now you might think that the right thing for me to do would be to show Tina how to open up the calculator on any computer, including her own—and you'd be wrong. That would be the incorrect thing to do. If anybody in this office had wanted Tina to know about such things, they'd have shown her already.

It wasn't my job to train anyone. I'd have gladly done it if it were part of my assignment; I like helping people discover better ways to do things. Yet, if I learned one thing working in the accounting office, it was to do only what was asked of me. Taking

161

on extra projects without permission only gets a temp in trouble. This gopher was going to keep his nose in his own hole.

"Must be beginners luck that I got the good computer," I told Tina with a humble smile.

"Jeez! Look how much you've got done," she replied, seeing all the filled in cells in the right column. She could not see the whole sheet, so she had no way of knowing that I had it all done. "I guess having the good computer makes a difference."

Now you might think that the right thing for me to do would be to show Tina how to write a simple spreadsheet formula and drag it down a column of cells—and once again, you'd be wrong. If showing her how to open the calculator was a mistake, this would be an error of catastrophic proportions. This would shake the college to its very foundations, and get me sent home before lunch for being a troublesome meddler.

As far as I could tell, there was no reason to believe that Tina couldn't learn how to use spreadsheet formulas just as well as I could, but I hadn't come here to make trouble. Tina and her co-workers had their routines, and they seemed perfectly happy in them. If their supervisors had wanted them trained in different things, I assume their supervisors would have trained them. "Is that a lot?" I asked, batting my novice eyelashes.

"Is that a lot?" she mocked. "Guess who's doing all of our math from now on?"

I guess that was a rhetorical question, because she hurried off to her friends before I could guess. She huddled up with Sherrie and the redhead. They looked at me as they talked. Tina said something emphatically. They all nodded and smiled. It looked like they were about to give each other high fives. Without hearing a word of it I knew that Tina had explained that they should shove all tasks involving math to the temp at the good computer in the back corner.

Tina's plan was actually a good idea. It was the most

efficient use of resources, and it seemed to raise office morale. These were not stupid women. It wasn't their fault that the institution of higher learning for which they worked gave no thought to training them. And as far as the math goes, if I were made to spend my day manually calculating averages from series after series of numbers, I would think it a horrible drudgery too. I would make no bones about passing it off to the temp.

I spent the rest of the day performing various feats of mathematical wizardry. The mathematics was all smoke and mirrors; the real wizardry was making it appear that it took me all day to do it. By the end of the day I was pretty tired. Doing math is one thing, but faking doing math can be quite taxing.

At different times, Rae came out of her office on inspection tour. She marched around barking orders at the three ladies, before strutting back to her office in perfect confidence that her will would be done. A few people came to meet with Rae in her office. Some of them looked very much as if they should outrank an executive assistant in the scheme of the college, yet they came to her. They came to her, and they treated her with a deference that seemed backward in its direction. Even with her door shut, it was clear that she talked louder, and with less diplomacy, than all of them.

It was interesting to see how the ladies in the outer office with me reacted to Rae's oversight. The redhead, whose name turned out to be Gail, was the most eager to please Rae. She nodded at everything Rae said, and was always on the lookout for clues that would tell her how high, so she wouldn't have to ask if Rae told her to jump.

Sherrie, the blonde southern belle, was different. She showed deference to Rae, but you could sense her secretly rolling her eyes and thinking, "You're still just a secretary," every time Rae exhibited her dominance. Clearly, Sherrie found Rae to be too big for her britches, but she also found her too big to openly defy.

Tina was somewhere in the middle. She didn't wait for the chance to jump at Rae's command, and she didn't roll her eyes. She reacted to Rae's supervision as a survivor. Fawning was as repugnant as subtle scorn was dangerous. She took the path that was sure to keep her out of Rae's dog house, and nothing more. Whatever her personal feelings toward Rae were, they were hidden beneath a facade that was all business.

Among the three of them, Gail, Sherrie, and Tina were akin to the amenities of the three little bears' cottage in regard to Rae. One was too soft, one was too hard, and one was just right. Rae was no Goldilocks though; she really liked being affirmed, so there probably wasn't such a thing as too soft.

We didn't catch sight of any college presidents that day, or the day after, or the day after that. I was beginning to get the idea that we never would. The way Rae strutted around like the cock of the walk, issuing orders and holding closed-door meetings, it looked like we might not need one. I began to suspect there was no President Burton. Sure, there was a portrait in the conference room with that name underneath, but the more I studied the likeness with all my imagination, the more it seemed like a hoax. You could clean up any bum and stick him in front of a camera. The guy in that picture probably fell off a freight car down at the depot. For the price of a nice suit of clothes and fifth of gin why wouldn't he suffer himself to be given a bath and have the occasion documented on film? He probably even kept a "wallet sized" with which to impress all his acquaintances on the Union Pacific line.

I was becoming convinced that the only President Burton in this town was the little man trapped in Rae's body. Whether he was trying to get out was anybody's guess. What was evident was that Rae wasn't about to let him go. He made her bold and brash, and she liked that. He gave her the gumption to grab hold of all the power she could reach. He might get out some day, but sure as hell, she was keeping his balls.

16.

If I'd Known Calculus Could be This Sexy, I Would Have Studied More

Gwen started getting used to the idea that I was back temping at Appalachian Downslope College. She consoled herself that it was better than having me not working at all. All notions of road tripping to see Elvis were dead and gone, and we'd be able to pay the rent at month's end. She must have found some comfort in that, because I could feel normalcy returning to our relationship. After a few more quiet weeks, everything would be good.

What a fine line there is between things that would be and things that would have been. It only took a couple of 11-year-old Polaroids to slip us over that line. Hence: after a few more quiet weeks, everything *would have been* good.

As for the Polaroids, Gwen shoved one into my face upon my arrival home after my third day at work in the president's office. "Who's this?" she asked. Her tone indicated that she was looking for more than a name; she was looking for a good reason why she should not throw a vase at my head.

"Good Lord!" I said, not because that was who was in the picture, but because the picture raised a myriad questions to my mind.

"Wrong!" she declared. "Try again."

"Where on earth did you get that?" I gasped.

"Nope! You get one more try," she said, eyeing the heavy glass vase on the corner table.

"That's Kelly Manchester," I said.

"Now we're getting somewhere. Next question: who the hell is Kelly Manchester and why do you have naked pictures of her?"

"Pictures? There's more than one?"

With her other hand she thrust another Polaroid at me, also Kelly Manchester, also naked.

"Good Lord!" I said again.

To be more precise about the photos, the Kelly Manchester in them was not completely naked. She was only very nearly naked. In each photo, she wore some little stitch of clothing that kept just enough mystery alive. For the record, I had never seen Kelly Manchester in anywhere near as little clothing as this, though at one time I had dearly wanted to. Now, in spite of the creek I was up, without a paddle, I found myself dearly wanting to again.

Perhaps I should explain my association with Kelly Manchester. Kelly was the *it* girl in my high school. She was cute, sassy, and popular, not to mention well-endowed. Like a lot of other guys in my class, I spent long periods of time convinced that I was in love with her. That I was in lust with her took no convincing. There was plenty of involuntary proof of that.

Kelly didn't have to be nice to anybody, but she was always friendly to me. I couldn't figure out any particular reason for this, so one day, after calculus class, I decided to test a theory and ask her out. She was compassionate, and let me down easy, explaining how busy she was the weekend I had in mind. I suggested some other time, as a honorable retreat from the predicament into which my presumptuousness had led me. She agreed to the open-ended timetable, whereupon I ran away to lick my wounds.

Kelly was gracious, and acted as if the incident never happened. I was grateful for that. She could have humiliated me by advertising my foolhardy attempt to date so far above myself. Having been let off the hook, I decided to let that dog lie and not bother Kelly with silly requests anymore. At least I now knew that she wouldn't go out with me, and I could die with my chin up, knowing that I had tried.

I still spent most of the time in calculus class with my chin in my hand, sighing and staring at Kelly. I still had dreams about her, asleep and awake, but I never again entertained the belief that any of those dreams could come true. After graduation we went our separate ways. I have not seen her in years.

"You wanna talk, or you wanna walk?" Gwen asked, snapping me out of my teenaged reverie. I could tell by her tone that she was not referencing any kind of walk that would lead me back to this house at the end of it. Therefore, I opted to talk.

"Honey, I swear, I have no idea where those photos came from." This was the absolute truth. You could not have picked something that I expected to come home to less than photos of a nearly naked Kelly Manchester.

"Why?" she asked. "Did you forget where you hid them?"

"I never hid them anywhere. I've never seen those before in my life."

Gwen was making no progress in this direction. She changed lines. "So who is this tart, this Kelly Bigchested, anyway?"

"Kelly Manchester was a girl from my high school. I haven't seen her twice since graduation, and I've never seen her *like that*."

"Did you date her?"

"No." I didn't feel it was wise to mention any of the back story.

"Why not? She looks like quite a little good-time girl."

"Kelly Manchester wouldn't have lowered herself to date somebody like me. She was out of my league."

167

"Then how did you get her amateur porn pics?"

"I don't know. I didn't know I had them. Where *did* I have them?"

"Hidden where I would never find them," she scoffed as she nodded toward a book setting on the couch.

I picked up the book. It was my high school calculus text. As a man who is with the one woman he wants to marry, I am not proud of what I felt when I recognized the book, but I'm trying to tell the whole story. I felt remorse. I was not remorseful because I had naughty pictures of a classmate in my textbook; I was remorseful because, for all these years, I had not realized that I had naughty pictures of a classmate in my textbook. I was most remorseful of all because I went through the last few months of my senior year without knowing that I had naughty pictures of my fantasy girl in my textbook. Perhaps I should have studied more.

It came flooding back. It was maybe two or three weeks after I had unsuccessfully asked Kelly out. She borrowed my textbook one day, which I thought was kind of weird because I imagined she used the book as little as I did. Maybe I was re-writing history, but I seemed to remember that she had a peculiar smile on her face when she handed it back to me. If I had only been more curious I would have done better in school, in more ways than one.

The book, bearing the weight of missed opportunity, lay heavy in my hands. "She must have slipped them in the day she borrowed this," I muttered. I was not explaining to Gwen; I was bringing myself to terms with a tragic loss.

Gwen misread my lament as defense. "So you're saying this chick slipped you some homemade glam shots on the sly, huh?"

"What?" I'd forgotten what year it was, and that there was a third person in the room with Kelly and me. "Oh. Yeah. She did."

"And you expect me to believe that?"

"Yeah. I do."

"Okay. I believe it. Not because you necessarily deserve to be believed, but because it does kind of explain these notes at the bottom of the pictures."

Curiosity that I should have had in twelfth grade snapped my head around toward Gwen. "What notes?"

"Well, let's see. The picture in which the boobs are the prominent feature says, 'I think you're really cute.'" Gwen slid the top picture behind the other one in her hand. "And the butt shot says, 'You should ask me again.'" She looked up at me. "Ask what again?"

Now that I had Gwen on the path to believing me about the big picture, I didn't want to mess it up by fibbing about the details. "I'm not positive, but I assume it means ask her out again."

"Ah ha! So you did ask her out."

"Yes, and she said she was busy. I thought she was being nice and letting me down easy."

Gwen let out a devilish giggle. "Oh, if you only knew. What a kick in the balls these must be." She waved the Polaroids in the air. "Should have cracked the books. I bet you didn't do very well in calculus class either."

"Here, let me see those notes." Gwen gave me the pictures without a fuss. They would punish me more than she ever could. In the white space beneath each photo were the exact words she'd read, written in the effusive script of a teenage girl.

"Wow, that's gotta ache," Gwen remarked as she watched me stare at the long-lost overtures.

It did ache. If you're a guy who didn't get much action in high school, you'll know exactly what I mean. Sure, I'm intimate with a very attractive woman now, but that fact doesn't have the same impact as it would have had in high school. Hooking up with Kelly Manchester could have been a seminal moment in my development. For that average high school boy, a romance with a girl the likes of Kelly Manchester was reaching for the stars. I would never have that high school boy chance to reach for those stars again. It was done, over, gone forever. Looking at those pictures of Kelly was like finding a winning lottery ticket you'd forgot about in your other coat until it was expired. Those numbers would never line up like that again.

Gwen had lost her edge of anger. She was not quite ready to show compassion for my loss though. She was quite ready to mock compassion. Sitting down beside me, she petted the back of my head. "Poor little guy," she cooed. "Didn't get his big chance to bang the school slut."

I stared at the photos. Thinking about how hot the high school Kelly Manchester was helped me ignore Gwen's faux pity.

I must have shaken my head too earnestly at her mention of my loss, because Gwen lost her patience for mockery. "Oh, come off it!" she huffed. "You know that girl was an STD factory, don't you?"

"Yeah, probably was," I said with a quiver in my voice, but I didn't believe it for a second. Kelly Manchester had saved all of this sexiness for me alone. These photos were taken with only me in mind. Of course they were.

"She probably put these little souvenirs in the books of every boy in your class."

"Likely," I agreed, though it was impossible. These were the only pictures of this nature that Kelly had ever taken. I could see it in the eyes of the lovely girl in the photograph.

"In fact," Gwen went on, "a girl like that's probably been so used and abused by now that you wouldn't even recognize her anymore." I nodded, though I was sure it wasn't true. "It's too bad really, because even I have to admit, she was pretty hot." My ears perked up. The commentary had taken an unexpected turn. "You know, I'm not really into girls that much, but if I were, I'd have to give a girl like that a second look."

I might have found some consolation in the fact that Gwen thought I had good taste in dream girls, but I could not. The idea that Gwen found Kelly sexy was torturous. It sent through me a thrill at the possibilities; then it reminded me that all those wonderful possibilities were long past any hope of fruition. Gwen had merely grabbed hold of my natural male perverseness and twisted it till it ached. It was my punishment for being a naturally perverse male.

Gwen made a few more over-the-top comments about how firm Kelly's body was, but I wasn't listening anymore. I guess it was good that she wasn't really angry about finding the photos, but she was wasting everybody's time by trying to rub it in. Sometimes women just don't understand that fate doesn't need their help when it kicks a guy in the nuts.

No matter what Gwen said now, I was a haunted man. I was haunted by the shadows of things that might have been, and I always would be haunted by them. By all appearances, I would get over this. I would seem to live the normal life of a man who was satisfied that he had tried his best, but largely failed, at being a teenage boy. But sometimes, late at night, I would toss and turn, knowing that the success of my wildest dreams had lain only thinly veiled behind my failure. Gwen would not know my thoughts then. She would neither console nor chastise me. Fate was my true punisher.

Now, some of the women out there might not have much sympathy for my regrets. In fact, they might think that those regrets paint me as a real jerk, because they indicate that I would trade the wonderful woman I have now for the hot teenager in the pictures. Those are the women that don't understand the male mind. I do not want to trade Gwen for the young, supple Kelly Manchester. I don't in the least want to give up Gwen; I want them both. That is to say, I want to have done my thing with Kelly when

I had the chance, and I want to be right where I am with Gwen now.

The way I look at it, the two are independent of each other. If I'd gotten together with Kelly in high school, I would certainly have more fond memories of those years, but I would have ended up right about where I am. Any romance between Kelly and myself was not destined to outlive high school. We were very different people with a world of disparity between our aspirations. Everything from the day I went to college would have been exactly the same, except that I may have walked a little taller and spoken up a little louder when the guys were boasting about their high school exploits.

If fate had not been quite so cruel to me, I'd still be living with Gwen, and I'd still be working at Appalachian Downslope College. You'd think making me work at Appalachian Downslope College would be cruelty enough to satisfy fate, but I guess not. The only thing that would be different today, if I'd been allowed to indulge in a real life schoolboy fantasy, is that I would have moved those photos from my old calculus book to a much more secure location, where Gwen would never find them. And even if she did find them, it would just go to prove that I'm a guy who does own a little mojo after all, and knew a thing or two about wooing pretty girls before she fell out of the sky and into my life.

Well, that's what I wanted. What I got was a girlfriend who was getting sick of watching me agonize about missed sexual opportunities in my past. All the sighing and head shaking I was doing must have finally gotten to her. "Okay," she said. "Pity party's over. Let me have them." She held out her hand toward the photos. "They're not going to do you any good anymore."

I held out the pictures and she took them. Well, she took them eventually. She had to tug at them a few times before she got them pried from my grasp. I didn't put up too much resistance though; a whimpering man never does.

She started to throw the pictures in the trash but stopped short. "Maybe I ought to throw these out somewhere else," she said. "We can't have you digging through the garbage like a hungry puppy."

"Thanks for being so considerate of my reputation," I replied. "It's only a huge part of my youth that you're tossing out so carelessly."

She laughed. "You wish! Face it, Gary. This girl was just about as much a part of my youth as she was yours. It's over. Let it go. You're only going to sprain yourself getting all worked up over memories of something that never happened." She came to me and took my face in her hand. She kissed me with her tongue. I don't know what she did with the pictures, but they were no longer in her hands. With her hands she was touching me very rightly. "If you're going to get yourself all worked up, do it in real life," she whispered. She was right. Making love to Gwen was so much better than not having made love to a high school girl.

The new perspective Gwen gave me helped get me over the photos of Kelly Manchester. I have not seen those snapshots again. I knew I would never see them again, so I didn't bother looking for them. On the whole, that was okay with me. As long as Gwen was willing to snap me back into reality every so often, I could forgo fantasy. That doesn't mean that I didn't secretly go through all my other old textbooks though. Just in case there were any long lost pictures lurking around, I thought it was worth a look. It wasn't that I was looking to lament any other missed opportunities, but I figure a guy should make every attempt to learn the most accurate history of himself. I didn't find any more hidden treasures. That was probably a blessing, because if I'd found similar photos of other girls I probably would have seriously sprained myself before Gwen could administer first aid.

173

17.
Napoleon's Urinal or How I Met My Water-Loo

One day a railway hobo walked right into the president's suite at Appalachian Downslope College. This was not a case of socio-economic profiling on my part. I knew he was a hobo because I knew that he was a *particular* hobo. I had seen his picture hanging on The Wall of College Presidents. He was the transient that Rae had hired to impersonate President Burton.

He was rather more stout than tall, and reasonably well groomed, in the suit that Rae had provided him; still, it was clear to the astute observer that he was a complete hoax. His jacket was both too tight and too long for him. His tie was hideous and clashed with every other article about him. Its multitude of colors co-existed only through an awkward truce with each other, and they certainly were not capable of living in peace with anybody else. This man's entire wardrobe had been selected and applied by somebody who did not love him.

As one drew nearer to him, it became apparent that he had been doused in cheap cologne to cover his indigenous odors. His eyes were foggy and he seemed to lack the capacity to focus them. He looked all about him as he walked, but it was difficult to say if he actually noticed anything. He looked right through me, as if I were as meaningless as an empty bottle. He waddled just a little bit as he moved on his legs. This was the only thing that puzzled me. I couldn't see how he could catch up to a rolling box car with such an inhibited gate. Still, I was convinced of his true identity.

The ladies in the outer office showed great deference as

they wished President Burton a good morning. I couldn't tell if they were just playing along, or if Rae had them all hoodwinked. The imposter didn't seem to care. He mumbled something at them and disappeared into the office marked as the president's. He immediately closed the door, which no doubt allowed him the privacy to kick off those uncomfortable city-slicker shoes and toss back a couple swigs of breakfast.

I have to say that for a man plucked from skid row, this President Burton character could display a fair amount of charisma. After a couple of hours of rest, he emerged from his office and began interacting with the world. That is not to say that he had any noteworthy contact with me, or any of the ladies of the outer office; he saw them as necessary obstacles between himself and the doorway; he took no note of me at all.

He did interact with certain members of the college who came in from outside. In the bits of these interactions to which I was privy, this man proved himself quite an actor. He smiled and pumped visitors' hands, and coolly blew smoke up whatever garment covered their legs, like a real-life college president. He might have convinced me that he really was one of the latter class, had not Rae made a point to hawk over him during every exchange.

If this faux President Burton had reached his prime in an earlier era, he might have made an excellent snake oil salesman. On the other hand, he probably would have turned around and spent all his profits on the next confidence man's snake oil. For every puff of smoke he blew up some outsider's leg, Rae blew an equally jolly puff up his. Maybe he needed his supply of smoke replenished, but Rae didn't. She just kept chugging away with her endless supply.

For as polished an actor as he was, I couldn't help thinking that Rae must be giving away the hoax with the tactless way she tugged at his strings. Did no one wonder why they could not beg,

175

borrow, or steal a private word with the college president? If anyone questioned her constant imposition between the boss and his business, they did so privately. Either these people were universally dense, or they genuinely feared the power behind the throne. It could easily be the former, but then if you crossed your eyes just so, Rae really could be the spitting image of Mussolini.

Much like Mussolini, Rae had a reputation among the girls of the outer office for making the proverbial trains run on time. "She's really a wiz with computers," Gail had told me. Though I may have suspected mere sycophancy from Gail, Tina and Sherrie backed her up. They all agreed that Rae knew her office software inside out. These testimonials soon gave me some insight into the rise of Mussolini. As it turns out, sometimes making people believe that the trains are running on time is as simple as hiding the railway schedule and announcing the promptness of each train's arrival whenever it happens to reach the station.

In the afternoon, after several days of having lived happily oblivious to my existence, Rae called me into her office. She had become dissatisfied with the white index tabs on the many hanging file folders in her cabinets. She would be so much more pleased if they were all yellow instead of white. She didn't say it, but I got the message that she would also be pleased to teach the new guy the extent of her power over him by making him spend his entire afternoon performing the mind-numbingly tedious, and equally needless, task of remaking all of her index tabs in yellow.

Since mind-numbingly tedious, and equally needless, is the bread and butter of the average office temp, I had no grounds on which to be dissatisfied with the task. This was clearly the type of task that called for a half-assed job. While I was deciding which half of my ass to put into it, Rae, the micro-manager, stepped in to help me. The files, it turned out, were too confidential to leave her office. Therefore, I was to make a written list of all the labels, before going out to print up new ones on yellow tabs. Then I would come back and take each old label out of its little plastic sleeve and replace it with the identical, yet more festive, label. I was pretty sure there was nothing of interest to anyone in any of those files. Rather, Rae wanted to watch me suffer through writing out the list.

I began listing the names of Rae's hanging folders with a good, stout half-heartedness. The joy she felt at making me menial ebbed as the tedium of my work spread itself to my audience. Eventually, she turned her attention back to the work on her monitor. She was quiet at first, but grew louder as the minutes passed, apparently frustrated with something that was not working out well for her. Before long, she was huffing and puffing at the screen. Soon, I was taking time out of my tedious schedule to enjoy watching her struggle at her work.

She almost caught me enjoying her troubles when she turned toward me. "You there, boy," she said. She may not actually have said those words, but the tone she used to get my attention was so condescending that it meant, "You there, boy."

"What, me?" I asked, as if there were any other young, male pups in the room.

"Yes, you. Do you know how to split a person's name into first and last in two separate cells?" From what I saw on her screen, it was clear that she was talking about a range of names on a spreadsheet.

"Yeah," I said. "You have to split text to columns."

"Of course I do. But it's been so long since I've done it, I'm having trouble remembering the procedure. Come here. Refresh my memory."

It turned out she wasn't quite the wiz the girls outside thought she was. I couldn't really hold that against her though. Everybody likes to make people think they're smarter than they are. As long as she knew a bit more than the rest, she was all the wiz she needed to be. This explained the dearth of training

177

provided to the ladies of the outer office. I went over and boldly took hold of her mouse. "How do you want your cells delimited?" I asked as I began pointing and clicking.

She paused to let the wheels in her head spin. When they got up to speed, she replied. "The normal way."

"Commas?" I asked.

"Yes. I think that's what I used last time I did it."

As I innocently went on talking her through the process, her eyes narrowed more and more. I took no notice of this at first, as I was caught up in a callow moment of trying to be helpful. I only noticed the changes in her face at the point when I was about to make the last click that would accomplish the function. I saw the dark, calculating cynicism in the slits of her eyes, and I knew I had walked into a trap.

Of course she was getting me to show her something she did not know, but she was also testing me. She was not a subtle lady; her methods were conspicuous. Therefore, I should have known better. There was a reason no one under her authority was very skilled at office software. However skilled, or not, Rae really might be, she must appear to be greatly more skilled than those around her. I was on the point of proving myself the exception to her rule, and that would be the end of my tenure in the president's office.

I clicked the wrong option. The operation failed. "Hmm," I said, making disappointed faces. "I could swear this is the way the instructor in my training session did it."

"You've never done it on your own?" she asked.

"No," I lied. "But it looked so simple when they were showing us how to do it in class. Maybe we shouldn't have used commas." I began clicking around her application, mumbling advice to myself and acting more and more frustrated. "Darn it," I sighed. "I know we're real close. I'm sure there's just one little thing messing us up, but I can't remember what I'm doing wrong."

After I had clicked around wildly enough to make her fear for the parts of her sheet that did work properly, she wrested the mouse from my hand. "Maybe you should leave this to me and go back to more manageable tasks," she said, nodding toward the files.

In the flash of brilliance that the moment required, I stared a blank stare at her. I held it long enough for her to conclude to herself that I was just the overreaching dolt that she needed me to be. "Go on," she nudged. "Get back to your files."

I started to go, but I held my stare, to reinforce to her that I was poorly skilled and below average in intelligence. These being my official characteristics, my place within Rae's empire was more secure.

If Rae got to enjoy making me sit in the corner and do menial tasks, I got to sit in the corner and watch her compound her frustration at not being able to arrange her list of names the way she wanted. I was concerned that she would follow the path I had laid out and eventually stumble upon the last correct move. But she showed little interest in following that path. I must have sold my incompetence so well that she figured I had been on the wrong path all along. Or it could be that she was just not very teachable. At any rate, she went back to square one and stumbled around in the dark, making ever louder grunting noises. Eventually, she gave up and sorted her list alphabetically by first name, which I'm sure was pretty useful.

Rae was so wrapped up in her frustrations that she forgot all about me sitting in the back corner of her office. I was taking my own sweet time making my list of her files, curled up on the floor in a nice little nook, with warm sunshine coming through the back window. If I'd had a couple of boxes I could have made a nice little fort. With a decent pillow I could have had a nap.

Someone knocked at the door. From where I lounged, I couldn't see who came in, and I didn't really care to crane my

179

neck to look. From the voice, I surmised that it was the lead male actor in Rae's little comedy show. I expected Rae to kick me out, but she really had forgotten about me. They pitched right into their discussion. It was already too late to remind them of my presence by coughing or slamming closed a file drawer. I didn't lament that missed opportunity. After all, it wasn't *my* job to keep track of me. I was innocently garrisoning my little fort, which was just exactly in compliance with my latest orders.

Rae and her stooge were having a debate about removing the head of the history department. From what I gathered, there were three people who could be considered for department head. The first was the incumbent, who by some unaccountable means, rose to the position because she merited it. She had no supporters in the discussion. The second candidate was the one championed by the artist known as President Burton. He earned that support by being a guy who "keeps everything in its place and doesn't try to do things." Rae's candidate was even more pliable. Not only did he not rock any boats, he treated Rae with deference above any that the typical faculty member would pay the typical executive secretary. Rae didn't come right out and say it, but what she meant was that her man understood the power structure of the college and was willing to live with it.

For a mere pawn, President Burton was pretty feisty in his argument. Who would have guessed that a hobo would care so much about who was head of the history department? He almost had me believing that he might be a real college president, until I asked myself why a real college president would spend so much time arguing with his secretary over something like this. I finally concluded that Rae had spruced up the wrong transient; consequently, she found herself stuck with a figurehead who lived and breathed the role.

I was getting tired of my fortress of solitude. The sun was starting to get hot, and my butt was weary from resting on the floor. Yet I dared not stand up. To stand up was to show myself, and to show myself was to become unemployed again. A temp who'd seen the seedy inner workings of any institution was an endangered species, and Rae wouldn't bat an eye at any creature's untimely extinction. Hence, my task became a half-assed job in the literal sense, as I shifted my weight from one cheek to the other to ease my discomfort.

At length, the debate reached a stalemate. The only thing that had been decided was that the deserving incumbent would be removed, as she could not be counted upon to do anybody any favors. The identity of the replacement was still uncertain. This is when Rae played a gambit that I imagined she had used often. "Remember, a couple of weeks ago, when you came up with the idea that whoever chose the next department head should also be the one who had to deal with keeping them happy, and field all their complaints?" she asked her president.

"Not really," he replied. "Did I say that?"

"Of course you did. I remember telling you how much sense I thought that idea made."

He made thinking noises. "Well, it does make good sense. It was a pretty good idea I had."

"It was, but then, you can always be counted on for a good, sensible idea. Like when you decided that it would probably be better if I had to deal with all the grief from the new head, because, as you said, you are really too busy for all that nonsense."

There was a pause, during which I half expected him to rebel against the expressions of good sense that were being attributed to him. I suppose he did not want to appear to be arguing with his very sensible self, so he went along. "Well, yes, I am too busy to waste time coddling a new department head. Maybe it's best if I leave this all to you."

I could actually hear Rae struggling to hold back her grin of triumph. "You're nothing if not consistent," she told him.

"That's almost exactly how you put it last time this issue came up."

"And I don't even remember that I said it. So it's like I had two, separate great ideas," he proclaimed, taking pride in his supposed consistent far-sightedness.

"It just goes to show your skill," Rae fawned. She cleared her throat, presumably to flush the treacle out of it. "So, I'll just take care of this whole matter. You don't need to waste another moment on it."

"Good. That's what I was trying to get at all along." I heard him get up. "I'm glad I was able to bring you around to my way of thinking without too many bumps." The door opened and closed, whereupon Rae spent a good minute chuckling.

It was all so odd. I couldn't figure out why Rae spent so much time outflanking her lead actor when she could just direct him in the scene. It argued for him being a real college president who only acted like a wino. But if that were true, why would he even allow himself to get into debates with his assistant? That argued for him being a real wino who discovered that he had the power to expose his puppet master's scheme if she didn't allow him to pretend to the full extent he wished. It was very confusing, but so far I didn't have enough evidence to overturn my original assessment of their relationship.

The other thing I couldn't figure out was how I was going to get out of Rae's office without reminding her that I had been present for the entire discussion. Rae did not appear to be going out anytime soon. She just went back to playing with her enemies list, or whatever it was she'd been working on, with the difference that she was much more self-contented than she had been before her meeting. She kicked off her unflattering shoes and exposed her even more unflattering feet, making it clear that she was not anticipating a trip outside of her lair.

It was getting near the end of the day, which might have

given me solace, except for what I had already learned about Rae. Everyone in the suite agreed that she had no life outside work. She typically stayed in the office well into evening and often showed up on weekends. This was not out of character for someone who had come so near her goal of world domination. Any two-bit dictator could tell you that you can't fall asleep on your iron fist. You've got to keep it constantly out and about, where people can see it. And you've got to burn the midnight oil making sure no one else is burning more midnight oil figuring out how to unscrew your fist from your arm as you sleep.

Therefore, the only thing that the close of business brought was the chance for me to waste a big chunk of my free time bottled up in my corner hideaway. I couldn't wait her out. I had to act.

There was only one way out of the room, and that was the door on the other side of Rae's desk. If Rae had been just a little bit neater, I would have had no hope of escaping. There would have been no way to get by her desk without revealing my presence. My saving grace was a rolling cart, piled high with notebooks and papers, parked right beside Rae's seat. This might give me the cover I needed, provided I crawled in tight against it. This meant that I would have to pass within three feet of Rae in order to have any hope of sneaking by her.

None of this addressed the problem of how I was going to pass through her closed office door. I might not be able to pull off that pseudo-miracle at all, but I wouldn't know for sure until I'd gotten closer to the door and could get a lay of the land in front of the desk. It might have been more prudent to stay where I was until Rae finally decided to go home. But that would certainly cost me a big chunk of my evening, without any compensation, and that is high price to pay for someone who gets no vacation time or health insurance.

I lay down on the carpet and began the slow, painstaking crawl. At first it was easy, as far as my knowledge of commando crawling goes. When I started to come near the cart, it became more taxing. I had to cut as close to the cart as I could without touching it. I had to move silently, yet quickly enough to keep my legs from dangling out behind the cart for an excessive length of time.

I took care to be conscious of every move of my body, and still my elbow brushed the wheel of the cart. I didn't think it made a noise, but I could not be sure it didn't jostle the papers on top. I pressed myself flat, my head very near the side of Rae's desk. She stirred.

I heard her squeaking in her chair, even as her meaty right foot rose from the carpet. With my head nearly scrunched under the side of her desk, I watched that foot as it moved through the air toward my face. Seconds turned to hours as that oversized collection of toes hovered nearer and nearer. At last it began its descent, in a trajectory that threatened to bring it down upon my nose. Without making noise, I could only wiggle my head backward on the carpet, millimeters at a time. I compensated by drawing my lips back tight against my teeth, and making every effort at the unlikely task of retracting my nose.

As slowly as the foot came down, my movements were retarded even more. I closed my eyes and tried to eat my cheek. My cheek proved too durable and my eyes too frantic for my efforts. They flew open just in time to see the behemoth crash to earth. It had missed me, but at its angle of decline it actually left the little toe under my nose. My downward-looking eye registered the shock waves of the crash as they pulsated through the fleshy outer layers of the foot.

For all the horror of it, I remained unscathed. I breathed a sigh of relief, which was the last thing I should have done. Not only did that invite the odor of the sweaty, unholy thing into my nostrils, the draft of my breath caused a disturbance in the soft, white hair on Rae's toe knuckles. Between my urge to gag, and the twitch that shook her gruesome ankle, I thought all was lost. But I held in my bile, and her ankle came harmlessly to rest. I was safe for as long as I could hold my breath.

I immediately went to work at inching my head back. I had made some good progress at this and was feeling more secure when the toes sprang to life. They began, as individual entities, to dig and nestle their respective ways into the fibers of the carpet. I almost gasped aloud when I noticed the black globule of goo stuck between two of the toes. The only way to calm myself was to firmly conclude that this must be nothing more than a sweat-soaked piece of lint. Meanwhile, I redoubled my retreat.

When I had held my breath as long as I could, I relented and took a new breath. The sample was amply tainted with foot stench, but there was enough oxygen to sustain me until I could crawl a little farther away. My progress toward the door remained painfully slow, but each new breath I took held a lesser prospect of knocking me out from either the fumes or the horror of that awful set of toes.

At last, I wiggled my way before the door. I was crestfallen to find that it was closed tightly. In order to slip through it, I would have to reach up into plain sight and pull on the handle. If I could do that, I might be able to scoot through undetected.

There were many dangers involved with reaching up for that door handle. I could not see Rae's face from my spot on the floor, so I would not know when the best moment to reach would be. The handle might make noise. The door might creak. Any of the necessary movements might attract Rae's attention. Still, I was caught in no-man's land. I could not stay put; I could not retreat, least of all with the image of those demon feet still fresh in my mind. Just as it was for the 20th Maine at Gettysburg, the only viable option was to charge ahead.

I took a deep breath and raised my hand out of hiding, toward the unreasonably high door handle. I could have sworn that handle was crawling up the door away from me. Every moment I expected to hear the noises of Rae going to battle stations, as she noticed the body-less hand rising from the void before her desk. My fingers came very close to the handle, and still the silence held. In just another instant, my hand would be on the lever of my escape.

The handle began to turn, which would have been a great relief had my hand been on it. Since my hand was still an inch below, this meant that someone was wiggling it from outside. I yanked my hand down. Somebody knocked at the door. I heard Rae's voice say "Come in."

I was caught out in the open. There was nothing I could do to hide. All I could do was roll to the side so that the opening door did not hit me in the head. This I did without hesitation. The door barely missed me as it swung inward. I looked up to satisfy my curiosity as to who was to be the instrument of my undoing. If God had been with me, it would have been Sherrie, or even Tina. But, of course, it turned out to be Gail. It had to be the one that would do anything to win favor with Rae. I would be ratted out the moment she saw me.

If there were any good news, it was that she hadn't seen me yet. Standing there, almost on top of me, she was so rapt in making meaningful eye contact with Rae that she had not bothered to look down at the wretched creature at her feet. I stayed still. She was asking Rae for some instruction. Maybe if Rae answered her in a succinct manner she would back out of the room without ever looking down.

Rae had been terse before, and curt, but I'd never known her to be succinct. The conversation dragged on. I didn't even hear what they were saying, so focused was I on staying still and sending vibes to prevent Gail from looking down. At last I heard Gail thank Rae for her time. Gail took a half step backward and began to pull the door after her. She had never looked down.

186

Perhaps I would survive this after all.

"Gail. Wait a minute," Rae commanded. Gail and the door both stopped. "Have you ever heard of a spreadsheet operation called something like 'text to columns'?"

"Text to who?" Gail replied.

"I'm going to send you down to the computer lab and have them teach you how to do this one thing. Then I want you to come back and pretend like you're teaching me, so I can see if you learned it right." Then Rae spoke the words that were nails in my coffin. "Come here. I'll show you what it is."

Gail's first step came directly at my head. I squirmed and contorted, trying to make my head contract itself. I am convinced that I somehow made my head smaller by at least two hat sizes, because her toe should have poked me in the eye, but it didn't. It swept past, and even as I was breathing my relief, the toe lit harmlessly on the carpet. The heel followed the toe and would have touched down on the carpet as well, had my hand not been in the way.

I nearly bit my tongue suppressing the scream of pain. My only salvation was that Gail's heels were only half high. Otherwise, her shoe would have become one with my impaled hand. As it was, she merely lost her balance and fell into Rae's desk. In spite of my pain, I took advantage of the opportunity to crawl like the wind through the open door. Once outside, I leapt to my feet and jogged to the men's room for some cold water.

No amount of cold water could erase the square indentation on the back of my hand, or the red, swollen skin around it. If Gail had caught a glimpse of the impediment over which she'd tripped, even just enough to suggest that it were human, this wound would be incriminating. I wished to cover it up, but I dared not ask for a band-aid or anything that would make it more conspicuous. The day was almost over anyway. It was best to play it cool and not over-react.

When I got back to the president's suite, Gail was just coming out of Rae's office. I thought I detected a slight limp, but it could have been my imagination. What I didn't imagine was that Gail looked at me a long time. It wasn't what you would call a friendly look. I thought it spoke of suspicion. I put my hands in my pockets and went directly to my desk.

There were only about 10 minutes left till quitting time, but the way Gail was eyeing me from across the room made me feel too hot. I kept glancing toward Rae's office, expecting her to show up at the door, eyeing me with the same malice as Gail. Then, I imagined, they would close in on me, trapping me in their pincer movement of suspicion. When they made me show them my hands, the jig would be up. I couldn't wait them out for 10 minutes. I had to find sanctuary.

I fled back to the men's room. I figured I could just hide in a stall for 10 minutes and then go home. But there was no safety for me, even in the men's room. I walked in to find President Burton standing at a urinal. If he had been standing at the urinal like a normal guy, it would have been all right. I would have sped right past him into a stall and been safe. But he wasn't peeing like a normal guy. For lack of a better reference, it came to my mind that he was peeing like Napoleon. His legs were spaced wide apart. His hands, balled into fists, rested one upon each hip in the classic Superman pose. His chin was held high, as though he were addressing the adoring masses, even as he peed upon them. I even thought he swayed a little bit side to side, to insure that both his radiance and his water flowed to all the worshipers he saw in the white porcelain. He began whistling the tune of "Old Dan Tucker."

It was the whistling that stopped me short. It completed the tableau of his triumph at the urinal and provided more evidence of his true résumé. I must have made some noise in stopping, because he looked over his shoulder at me. If some unimportant person had come up behind Napoleon as he was addressing the empire, or

188

peeing at them, I guess Napoleon would have given that person the same murderous look that President Burton gave me. I'd interrupted his whole glory dream, and it was clear he didn't like it. The way he quit whistling and glared at me, it looked like he was about to take a swing at me, which in his present condition would have been a lot more swinging than I had the stomach for.

So I made a mistake. Instead of keeping my cool and continuing upon my way to the stall, I turned and left the men's room. Only after I'd left did it occur to me that nothing could look more suspicious. By my reaction, I had made the incident into a big deal. Rather than a guy who was innocently heeding the call of nature, I had made myself out to be the guy who got caught sneaking up on peeing Napoleon. It had not been a good day. For all my efforts to be harmless, I'd collected more potential enemies than a temp had any right to claim.

18.
My Work Here Is Done; Could You Please Sign My Time Slip?

That night I got to thinking that it might be a good time to call in sick, in spite of the day's pay it would cost me. Gwen pointed out that if I did that, I might show up the next day to find a new temp sitting at my desk. That was just another example of The Man always trying to keep me down, I told her. Gwen rolled her eyes. I took that as a sign of her support for my plight.

I told her the story of my day, which she found amusing and pitiful all at once. I showed her my wounded hand. She asked if I wanted her to drive me to the emergency room or just kiss it and make it better. I opted for the kiss, which was just as well because she wasn't exactly running for the car keys when she asked. She kissed my hand; it didn't really make it feel any better. It didn't do anything to remove the tell-tale indentation from it either.

Gwen thought the thing I had to fear most was that Gail had seen enough of me on her way down to be able to identify the blob on the floor. Though that was not unlikely, I had to disagree that it was the most dangerous event of the day. I can't make any woman understand this, but the most damaging thing was that I had seen the spruced-up hobo peeing the pee of the usurper. No man pees like that unless he is giddy with the knowledge that he has put one over on the world. Only men who have risen to heights they have no right to, and don't deserve, pee with such overbearing

190

triumph. A little Corsican peon, who has schemed and plotted his way to illegitimate power over an empire, pees like that. Also, an itinerant ne'er-do-well, who has been plucked from his own filth and cast as a figurehead, commanding the stupid saps who worked for their places, pees like that. He knows it, and I know, and unfortunately for me, he knows that I know it.

Gwen didn't really buy my theory about President Burton's humble beginnings. She thought there were too many obstacles to pulling off such an elaborate hoax. There would be too many opportunities for such a conspiracy to be unraveled. That may all be true, but she's never seen the great man pee. I have. I have seen the secret urinal gloating that no logical consideration of the facts can explain away.

The next morning I didn't see Gail or President Burton at all. I didn't think much of President Burton's absence. He tended to be out of the office a lot, leaving Rae to ply her will as he looked for signs of passing acquaintances down at the railway depot. Gail's absence disturbed me much more. She'd never been out since I'd begun working there. There could have been a million reasons why she was not there, but the fact that it happened to be the very next morning after she had tripped over me made me wary. I just wanted everything to be perfectly normal. I needed the peace of mind of seeing everyone and everything in their proper places.

I was so bothered by Gail's absence that I made a special trip to Sherrie's desk so that I could ask, "Is Gail sick today?" in passing.

"She's at some sort of computer training this morning. She'll be back this afternoon."

"What a relief." I let a sigh escape. Sherrie raised an eyebrow at me. "That she's not sick," I added. "Being sick is the pits."

"Nope. She's just at training, so you can relax. Though the

way she twisted her ankle yesterday, it's a wonder she came in at all."

I felt blood shoot to my face. "Oh, she twisted her ankle? I didn't know that."

"Yeah. She fell in Rae's office." I thought I detected the hint of a smile from Sherrie. "Tripped over some . . . thing. Fell right into Rae's desk. You didn't see her limping around?"

"No, I didn't. What did she trip over?"

I was sure that was a smile. "Didn't really say. All she said was that it felt like she had stepped on a jellyfish or something. You know, some sort of gooey invertebrate."

That's when I realized that my dented hand was hanging carelessly at my side, for anyone to see. I swung it behind my back. "Interesting," I said. "But I guess I should get to work."

I tried to keep my head down all day working on printing up Rae's new file labels. I felt a little more secure knowing where Gail was, but I still expected some of the voluminous shit that I had piled up around me to hit the fan at any moment. I was so distracted that I did not even fume over what a stupendous waste of time it was to make new file labels just because Rae was sick of the old ones. Why didn't she just have her office painted if she needed a change? I'd rather be painting the office than making these stupid labels. And why couldn't we just buy a bag of yellow, plastic sleeves to put the white labels in? I suppose that wouldn't take long enough for me to fully appreciate just how menial I was. Did I say I didn't fume over these things? Well, let's just say I didn't fume as much as I normally would.

President Burton rolled in just before lunch. He didn't give much notice to the ladies, but as he fumbled with his keys, he looked right at me. I wanted to look away, but no matter who he really was, in the game we were playing I had to avoid appearing to be disrespectful. So I met his gaze and tried to look innocent and amiable, as if I didn't know any dark secrets about him. It didn't work. His eyes narrowed and he ran his thumb across his throat. To everybody else it probably looked as if he were merely adjusting his tie. The gesture was smooth, very well veiled. But I got the message.

A minute later Rae called me and commanded that I come to her office. As much as things had deteriorated in the past 24 hours, I really hadn't mentally prepared myself for the end. I took a moment and did that now. I could be going home for good within the next five minutes. There was nothing I could do about yesterday. I could only be on my guard today.

"How are you coming with those labels?" Rae demanded as I stood inside her door.

"I'm making good progress," I replied. "There's a lot of them though."

"Keep working at them," she said. "I want them as soon as possible."

"I'll do my best."

Silence.

I expected her to get to the heart of why she called me in, but she said no more. I waited.

Had she forgotten that I was in her office again? This time I was determined to remind her before she burdened me with overhearing more of her dirty scandals. "Is there anything else?"

She looked up and frowned at me. "You still here? I thought I asked you to get to work on my labels?"

"I'm going right now." I slipped out.

I should have been relieved that she had not called me in to fire me. But I wasn't. Why did she call me to tell me to come into her office, only to tell me what she easily could have said on the phone? That's what I pondered as I sat staring at her stupid label template on my computer. It just seemed like another asinine idiosyncrasy until in dawned upon me that it was a meaningful idiosyncrasy. It was her tell. She had let her intentions slip through her poker face. Rae liked to look at condemned people, even if she had no intention of giving any hint that they were doomed. She was set on firing me. She only wanted to get her new labels done first.

Well, if Rae were intent on squeezing her new, colorful labels out of me before she gave me the axe, far be it from me to hold back on the labels. I was quite willing to work through my lunch to produce them.

Burton and Rae left for lunch together. Neither of them looked at me until they were out in the hall, whereupon Burton gave a glance back at me, as if to insure that they had a good head start and could lose me if I, for some unknown reason, tried to tail them. He also seemed to be under the illusion that I could not see him look at me through the glass. Rae didn't bother to look back. I guess she figured that if I tried to follow them, she would just hide out in the shadow of a doorway until I came by, whereupon it would be child's play for her to grab hold of my chin and snap my neck before proceeding on to her soup and salad.

When they were gone, Sherrie and Tina felt free to leave for their lunches. This left me in peace to complete Rae's labels. I had already completed her original order for labels. I ignored those and started over again. This time I inverted all the lettering so that the title of each file was spelled exactly backward. That would add a little mystery to Rae's cabinets.

Being undisturbed, and generally competent, the work went quickly. I was only interrupted by the return of Gail. She was uneasy at finding me alone in the suite. She almost fled altogether when she realized there was no on at hand to rescue her, should I slither to the floor and start clutching at her ankles again. She only needed to retrieve something from her desk, which she did by backing away from me the whole time. On her way out, she made it to within a few paces of the door before she broke into a trot.

Sherrie and Tina came back from lunch first. By the time

Rae and Burton came back, the two ladies were settled into their desks as if they had never heard of a thing called lunch. Tina had even set out a package of peanut butter crackers, just in case anybody wanted to believe her busy day left time for nothing more than a quick snack at her desk. After the safety of numbers had been established, Gail came back. She went straight to Rae's office. I couldn't help noticing that she checked the floor before sprinting in.

I was convinced more than ever that there was a conspiracy afoot. That conspiracy could not end well for me. I was sure enough of this to start taking action. I went over and stood between Sherrie's and Tina's desks. "How would you ladies like to be better with your computer software than Rae is?" I asked.

"We don't have time to take all those classes," Tina said.

"What if I could teach you right now?" .

"Why rock the boat?" Sherrie asked. "If Rae wanted us to know more, she'd have sent us to class. We're trained like she wants us trained. She gets snippy when people get ahead of where she wants them, and she's hard enough to take as it is."

She had a good point, but maybe I had a better one. "Here's why you should rock the boat." I tossed my head toward Burton's door. "One day that clown is gonna fall. This whole charade of his is going to be exposed and he'll be out on his ear. One day there'll be a new president, one that may just have a mind of his own. He'll need to select an executive assistant, and maybe he'll chose the one with the most skills, instead of the one with the most testosterone."

"I'm not so sure about that," Tina said. "He and Rae have a pretty tight grip on things around here."

"That's exactly why something has to break. If they were low key and played it cool, they could go on with this farce indefinitely, but they're so drunk with power that they're going to clamp down too tight, and eventually the whole thing is going to crumble in their hands."

"I don't know," Tina replied. "I'm not looking for trouble right now."

"What about you?" I asked Sherrie.

She thought about it for a minute. "How long would it take?'

"About half an hour."

"To teach me everything that Rae knows?"

"To teach you how to find out everything Rae knows, quickly and easily."

"Seriously? Well, I've got to see this. Show me."

I only showed her a few quick tips that I thought she could use in her everyday work. The bulk of the time I spent showing her how to use the help index and wade through all the gobbledygook to find useful examples to follow. Then I showed her how to search online message boards to find instruction from experts on just about any possible task she could ever want to do. She liked the idea that she could learn tasks as she needed them, which encouraged me to believe that she would actually use the resources I had shown her. Yet only time would tell if this stealth bomb I was planting would ever blow up in Rae's hands. The only thing that was certain was that I wouldn't be around to see it if it did.

After Gail came out of Rae's office, Rae called me in. Rae had a very comfy looking chair in front of her desk, but once again she did not invite me to sit. Instead, she started with: "Got those labels done?"

"Just now finished."

"You can start putting them on the files right away then."

"Okay." This time I gave her just a second to say anything else before I turned to leave.

"Oh, one more thing," she said, stopping me at the door. "When you were in here working on the files yesterday, I don't remember seeing you leave. When *did* you leave?"

"Oh, I don't know. I wasn't really keeping track of the time. I couldn't have been in here too long, though."

"It's no big deal," she said, with laughably transparent dishonesty. "Just one of those things. You know, when some little thing escapes your memory, and you have to try and place it, just because it's become a puzzle to you."

I nodded. "Yeah, that happens to me a lot. Just this morning I found myself racking my brain trying to remember who won the Super Bowl two years ago. I feel like I've considered every football team there is, but none of them seem like the right one. I must be missing somebody. It's maddening, isn't it?"

"Anyway," she continued as if I had not said a word, "you had to have left before my meeting with President Burton, because you weren't here when he came in, right?"

There are a lot of bosses in this world to whom I could have just confessed the truth right then and, in spite of the awkwardness, saved my job through the virtue of honesty. Rae eats those kind of people for lunch. "Yeah. No, I was gone before anybody came in."

"Then Gail came in and tripped over her own feet," she mused. "But I just can't remember seeing you go out."

"I'm pretty quiet when I'm focused on my work," I explained.

She actually took notice of me then. "What happened to your hand? That looks painful."

I winced. "Yeah, it still is bothering me quite a bit. Dog bite," I blurted.

"That's a weird looking dog bite, just one tooth mark."

"It's a pretty old dog. I don't think they take him to the vet that much. The kids feed him rocks. It's no wonder he's mean."

"Well, the sooner you start with those labels, the sooner you'll be finished," Rae said. That was as close as she was going to come to expressing condolences over my injury. I didn't mind. I was too busy finding amusement in a single piece of paper I spied on Rae's desk. It was a set of handwritten instructions on how to divide her spread sheet names into separate columns. They got a little vague half way down the sheet, where it became apparent that Gail had begun to lose interest.

I let myself be entertained by Gail's notes long enough that Rae had to clear her throat at me. She took my amusement as a personal affront. "The labels, Mr. Gray," she reminded me.

I retrieved the labels I'd printed and went back into Rae's office to install them. With all the evidence pointing to the fact that Rae was just waiting to get her new labels in place before firing me, one theory would have been to go really slow and drag the thing out for a day or two more. I could have done that, but I was pretty sure that the labels were only going to save me till the end of the day anyhow. I wasn't going to be invited back tomorrow regardless of how many of Rae's files were labeled. And if I went slowly, it would mean that only a fraction of her files would be arranged alphabetically by backward spelling, not all of them, as I intended.

I've done some ass-backward jobs in my career, and I've done some half-ass jobs, but to do an ass-backward job half-ass is one more ass than I can keep track of. You would think that it should be just as easy to alphabetize words that are spelled backward as words that are spelled correctly. It turns out it's not. There's something about seeing a series of words that look completely foreign that makes one question one's mastery of the alphabet. Consequently, it took longer than I had expected to replace the tabs on Rae's files. Also contributing to the slow going was the distraction of watching Rae try to interpret Gail's notes on how to do the spread sheet process she wanted to do.

Somewhere between Gail's processing and memorializing of instructions and Rae's interpretation of the results, there had been a breakdown. Rae went back and forth between the note pad and her computer, trying every possible variation of what Gail could have meant in her notes. At last, she picked up the phone and called Gail. I couldn't hear the conversation because Rae was making every effort to keep her voice low, but I could tell what was going on by the context I heard. The only words I heard clearly were when Rae lost control of her frustration. "No, I don't want you to just come in here," she barked. "I want you to just tell me what all this claptrap means!" Rae shocked herself into recognition of her own loudness. She shot an angry look at me. I held up a handful of yellow labels and smiled at her. Then I went back to concentrating on my work. I had made it a point of pride, despite the distractions, to finish the task by the end of the day.

I finished the job with a few minutes to spare, at which point I promptly announced the feat to Rae. For the first time, she seemed satisfied with me. Also, for the first time, she asked me to sit down in the chair before her desk. "All the labels are done?" she asked. I repeated that they were. "They're all in alphabetical order?" Instead of taking offense at the Kindergarten quality of this examination, I merely nodded and smiled.

"Good," she said. Her satisfaction bubbled up within her as she glanced from Gail's training notes to my indented hand. It overflowed her in the form of her next words. "We're going to have to discontinue using your services here."

Ignoring the fact that I needed the income, I continued smiling. "Okay, great," I replied.

Her satisfaction ebbed. "Do you understand what I'm saying? You're not to come back to work here."

"Yeah, I get it." I gave an ambiguous wink as I spoke.

"And you're not upset?"

"Not in the least." This was a bit of hyperbole. In fact, it was upsetting to be without a paycheck again, but I'd had a whole day to come to terms with that development, despite her belief that she was just now springing it upon me.

199

Her satisfaction was gone. "Why not?"

I leaned forward and spoke slowly. "Because my work here is done."

She looked aghast. "How dare you presume such a thing? I'm the judge of that!" she barked. "Your work here is done when I say your work here is done, and not a moment sooner."

"Well, is my work here done?" I asked.

She sneered and chewed upon some part of her own inner-mouth anatomy. "Yes, it is. And while we're at it," she didn't specify exactly what we were at, "let me give you a little heads up. You've got an attitude that won't serve you well. You think you're so smart, but you're not."

I waited for her to expound on that thought, or give examples of my not smartness, but apparently that was all she had. "Okay," I said. "Thanks for that info." I rose and opened the door. "I also have a little heads up for you. The filing system has been updated. 'Admissions Statistics' now starts with an 'S'. And so does 'Travel Expenses'." I went out and closed the door gently behind me.

After collecting the few personal belongings at my desk, I explained to the girls that this was my last goodbye. Sherrie and Tina expressed regrets, but Gail just kind of retreated to the background and looked as if she were afraid I was going to throw sharp pencils at her. Since the sharpener was all the way across the room, I just left.

In the hall I heard someone calling after me. Sherrie came running out. When she got close she whispered. "I've already learned how to do two new things. I'll be ahead of Rae at this by the end of the month."

"Or maybe noon tomorrow," I replied.

She thanked me and gave me a hug. For a second, I actually felt good about having worked there. I wished her well, and truly meant it.

200

So, you may still wonder whether I got fired for knowing too much about office software, or for hearing too much of Rae's private discussions, or for seeing too much in the men's room. Like you, I can only guess. My guess is that I got fired for any one of them.

19.
The Tentative First Draft of My Plan to Become a Grown-Up

That night, when I told Gwen that I had lost another job, she didn't get on my case at all. I think she knew that she had already made her point about not wanting me to keep working temp jobs; pressing the issue right then wouldn't help. She also got that there were very few things I could have done to keep that job. In spite of all my grand plans, it wasn't meant to be. So she didn't lecture me; she didn't even poke fun at me, which I know must have been difficult to avoid. She just sat with her arms around me on the couch and talked to me about happier things.

I think that was the moment when the pendulum within me started to swing back in the direction of wanting to try hard to make something of my life. My theory had always been that not trying hard would be more fun than trying hard. But I wasn't having too much fun. I wasn't having any fun trying to imagine where I would find my next paycheck. I wasn't having any fun entertaining the idea of not being able to pay the rent. And even if I could pay the rent, I wasn't having any fun thinking about making Gwen live like this indefinitely.

I love her. I love her more than anything. She deserves more than to wonder from day to day whether her man has a job. I want to marry her. I want the chance to test her concerns about how responsible a parent I will be. I want to prove to her that I wouldn't lose the baby in the course of my everyday errands. And

I want to prove it to her with our baby, the one she has already condescended to imagine having with me. I want to be able to support her and our baby, and have money left over for that 80-pound bag of dog food, just in case we find some use for that too.

I discovered that I do want to try hard. I want to try hard, not because I see my legacy as some dust-covered collection of intellectual properties, stored forever out of view of future generations. I want to try hard because I see my legacy as a kid who might just be a little proud of his dad, and who also is not malnourished or camping out under the stars year round. I want to try hard because Gwen deserves it from me, and if she can sell herself on having a baby with me, God bless her that moment of indiscretion, I'm going to let her do it.

I'm not sure how losing another temp assignment has brought me to the conclusion that I will buy Gwen an engagement ring first chance I get, but it has. I would have imagined that something much more romantic would bring me around to this. If my father had sat me down when I was a kid and told me: "One day, you're gonna lose a couple of shitty jobs in quick succession, and then you're gonna know you've met the woman you want to spend the rest of your days with." I'd have thought—well, actually, I'd have thought it was just another of my father's incoherent pieces of advice. I wouldn't have put much stock in it. And yet that's just what seems to have happened. Maybe I should reconsider some of Dad's predictions about life. All I need is a primer on the quatrains of Nostradamus to help decipher them.

I feel such a strong, strange feeling of readiness to marry Gwen that I am tempted to take my small savings and go buy the ring today. It wouldn't be much of a ring, but I'm pretty sure Gwen would appreciate it more than a postcard from Graceland. I'm not going to do it though. I'm going to resist the temptation because I want to give Gwen a better ring than I can afford right now. Also, I may need that savings to pay the rent, and though

Gwen won't care about the size of the ring, I guessing that she'd rather wait a little while than be engaged to a vagrant right now. So I'm determined to do the responsible thing and make her wait.

You're probably thinking, "He says he's ready, but in the next breath he makes excuses to put it off." Well, I can't prove you're wrong, but you are. Except for the part about where I'm going to acquire an income, I've never seen the future more clearly. I'm going to marry Gwen, and together we are going to work hard to provide a good life for our family. We're going to climb our way up the ladder and grab our own little share of the American Dream. Of course, just as we are about to get over the hump into living comfortably, Congress will raise the capital gains tax rate and our investment savings will be shot to hell, but we'll cross that bridge when we get to it.

It shouldn't sound like I'm making all of these high-flying resolutions without making any plans for seeing them through. I am making plans, sort of. The first thing I'm going to do is update my resume and do my best to make my assignments at Appalachian Downslope College sound as much like real jobs as possible. Granted, this will be an uphill battle, but I have an English major on my side. She's a wiz with action verbs. On top of that, I think I've proven that I'm no mere novice at administering a modest dose of hyperbole.

The second part of my plan is to avoid settling for another easy temp job and the associated slippage into complacency. This should be pretty easy, because after my recent history with my temp placements, I don't think either of the two agencies in town will be ringing my phone off the hook. By now they both probably have a black spot in their parking lots where the files containing my credentials were burned in various evil-cleansing rituals.

I have little doubt that I will find a job if I look hard enough. What that job will be, I have no idea. I have skills that could be useful in many different lines of work, and I generally don't develop a bad attitude until after the hiring process is completed. It seems like every time I got a temp assignment, and every time I lost one, Gwen would tell me, "Gary, you're way too smart for this." Well, now I guess we'll find out what I'm not too smart for.

Who knows, I may even take that drastic step and go for a master's. My experience temping at Downslope College has not completely soured me on that idea. This is as much a surprise to me as it is to you. Now that I've had a chance to step back and think about all the people I've met at the various places I've worked, I realize that there are Marge Mekos, and Steves, and Raes in every industry. I've met them all before, under different names and in different places. These three stand out only because I've never run afoul of their types in such close proximity to each other before.

In hindsight, I think Renee was right. The world of higher education is much like every other world. It has a system that plays to the advantage of the people on the top rungs of the ladder, just like every other industry does. That doesn't make the people at the top contemptible; it only makes them human. It's also a good incentive to start climbing. The inhabitants of the higher rungs of academia obsess about degrees no more than the bigwigs in retail obsess about sales. You really can't blame people for getting behind their product. I only hope I believe in whatever I end up selling just as much.

I think Gwen was right too. My frustrations had more to do with who I was than where I was. I was a temp, which is not what I am cut out for. My impulse is to pitch right in and start fixing things that I think need fixing. That's not really what's expected of a temp. In whatever kind of business they sent me to, I would have overreached and gotten myself into trouble. Sure, it didn't help that the luck of the draw plopped me down among the likes of Marge Meko, Steve, and Rae, but it wouldn't have ended well for me in any other organization either.

So, you see, I am capable of learning after all. Maybe I'm not as bad a student as I thought. Getting more education is, at least, worth considering.

Whether in school or the working world, I may not fall in love with the path immediately before me. My productive life could be a hard slog for a while, until I hit my groove. That's okay. I'm going to compensate for that with the final part of my plan.

The final part of my plan is to reap my joy in life from my family, even while it is imaginary. I intend to keep a constant eye on the spot in the grocery cart where the baby would be riding. Furthermore, I plan to never have to chase down a shopping cart/imaginary baby thief again, as I will make it a policy to discretely elbow any suspicious-looking women in the gut whenever they come within striking distance. And by the way, ladies, when it comes to the safety of my precious child, you're all suspicious-looking.

I think I'll be a good dad, even to the real baby. Clearly, I have no evidence to support this notion, but I feel confident in it. I think it has a lot to do with Gwen. Though she pretends to believe that I will drop the baby on its head at first contact, she wouldn't say such things if she really believed them. She wouldn't even imagine us having a baby together if she believed that. I know her. She would not have gone on a third date with me if she really believed that about me. Deep down, she thinks I'll be a good dad, and she's pretty damned smart, so I'm siding with her on that one.

When the real baby gets old enough, I suppose I'll have to sit him or her down and have that important talk. The one that begins: "Son or daughter, you're old enough to know the truth now. Back when your dad was much younger, and didn't know any better, he worked as a temp. But I want you to know, that doesn't make it right." Hopefully, the child will learn from my mistakes, instead of thinking that if they were all right for me to

206

make, they are all right for him or her to make too.

The only thing that gives me pause in my determination to marry Gwen is the fact that it would commit me to an annual appearance in her parents' Christmas card photo. That means spending more time with Doug and Lydia when they are at the height of their mania. On the bright side, I don't think I'll have to worry about Lydia giving me trouble. I think I've effectively neutralized her with my lakeside display. It will be years before she can look at me without getting the shakes.

I expect that Doug will always live in ignorance of his wife's secret shame, and therefore will hold me to a higher standard than I can hope to reach. The photo will merely be an annual report card where my failure is shown on my face. That's okay though. Fortunately, I have parents of my own, who taught me how to shrug off failure.

The baby will have to be in the picture too, I suppose. As far as I'm concerned, the imaginary baby is already in the photo we took at the lake. You just have to squint to see him, because he was born out of wedlock, and attempts were made to hide him behind the dog. Regarding the real baby: I will hate to have to put the poor child through that ordeal annually. I can only hope he inherits some decent coping mechanisms from his mother.

In fairness to the Goldblatts, I think they will be able to teach the baby things that I may not be as adept at. They can teach him about organization, schedules, goals, and things like that. They could turn out to be a useful set of grandparents to the little tyke. My parents will certainly adore the baby, but they will be suited only to teaching the same sorts of things they taught me. The more I think about this, the more I think it would be perfect if my parents could spend the bulk of their time with the baby when the child is asleep. I know that's not likely, but it would be nice, at least until the kid is old enough to realize how dangerous doing your own home wiring can be when all you know about electricity is based on hunches.

So, you see, everything is ready to fall right into place. I'll get a real job. The real baby will get love and learning from his various grandparents, according to their respective abilities. We'll have dog food on hand, in case we need it. All systems are go. The only little detail I need to make sure of is that Gwen is still interested in marrying me when I do present her with the ring.

I'd been growing a little worried about that lately. Let's face it: my prospects have been looking a little erratic. I haven't exactly proven myself to be a good provider. Gwen has shown that she can tolerate that sort of thing, when my liabilities affect only her. But when she has a child to consider, well, who could blame her for wanting more stability? That's the sort of thing a man should think about when he's lost his way and has to decide how serious he should be about finding it again. It's amazing how long it takes for it to get through to us though.

Today, I'm not nearly as worried about Gwen's response. My renewed confidence is built on a firm foundation. I had a dream. I dreamed that Gwen and I were bathed in starlight. She was dressed in flowing silks and moonbeams sparkled in her eyes. I didn't notice what I was wearing. I bent on one knee before her and pulled back the lid of the velvety box. For some reason, I held the box in a position from which I could not see the ring. But Gwen could see it. Her mouth hung open and her eyes widened. The expression was poetically vague; it could have represented any of a dozen different emotions.

"Gwen. My love," I said. "Will you marry me?"

I could see the word forming in her throat. I held my breath. Her lips parted.

That's when I passed out.

And the next thing I knew, I was awake in bed. The sun was streaming in through the window. Gwen was awake too. She was lying on her side, staring at me, with the biggest smile her face could hold.

"What's going on?" I asked.

"Nothing. I just had a really great dream."

"What was it?"

It was clear she didn't want to recount it to me. "Hard to describe. Just a really great dream."

She threw an arm around me and pulled herself close. She hadn't given up an inch of that smile.

The whole moment was really kind of freaky. But that's the kind of freaky I'll take without too many questions. Wouldn't you?

Made in the USA
Charleston, SC
06 December 2010